DEADLY
CODES

DEADLY CODES

A Gallagher Novel

JP O'DONNELL

iUniverse, Inc.

New York   Bloomington

iUniverse books may be ordered through booksellers or by contacting:

iUniverse
1663 Liberty Drive
Bloomington, IN 47403
www.iuniverse.com
1-800-Authors (1-800-288-4677)

Because of the dynamic nature of the Internet, any Web addresses or links contained in this book may have changed since publication and may no longer be valid. The views expressed in this work are solely those of the author and do not necessarily reflect the views of the publisher, and the publisher hereby disclaims any responsibility for them.

ISBN: 978-0-595-51411-3 (pbk)
ISBN: 978-0-595-50476-3 (dj)
ISBN: 978-0-595-61888-0 (ebk)

Printed in the United States of America

iUniverse rev. date: 02/13/2009

In memory of my parents: for showing me the way.

ACKNOWLEDGMENTS

I owe a special thanks to the following people who offered their assistance during the writing of this manuscript.

My preview readers: Diane Beane, Kristen Rzezuski, Britt Emery, Marcia Stein, Ellen Pollock, Phyllis Oblas, and Phyllis Melone. Thank you all for the many hours devoted to reading my work. Your comments have been invaluable.

William Schoendorf, a great friend and fellow golfer, who offered the technical support to make the story plausible.

My cousin, Lan. Your enthusiasm inspires me to keep writing. I think, by this time, I must owe you a distinctive, blue sapphire ring.

My wife, Ronney, for her editing skills of the early drafts and for putting up with me while I spent months in front of the computer.

Mr. L. Edward Purcell of the iUniverse editorial team for helping to bring my manuscript into its final form.

Keriann Golini, the beautiful young woman who posed for the cover.

Ana and John Turner of Studio 913 for their excellent photography.

My children, Jonathan and Randi. Your encouragement makes me strive to be a better writer.

Chapter One

Sometimes a simple decision can change everything.

It was the first Saturday in November, and the temperatures in the Greater Boston area were unseasonably warm. Jennifer Clark walked into the kitchen of her contemporary home in Newton Highlands and pulled back the black-and-white checkered curtains that covered the sliding doors leading out to the deck. As she opened the slider, she could feel the rush of summer-like air flowing in through the screen. This day was truly a gift of nature—an Indian summer morning worth relishing before the harsh winter weather settled in.

Jennifer and her husband, Bill, both in their mid-forties, had become empty-nesters during the past few months. Their two children, Luke and Marissa, were away at college. Luke was majoring in mathematics, hoping to pursue a career similar to that of his father, who was one of the top cryptographic analysts in the counterintelligence division of the National Security Agency.

Bill's position with the NSA required a considerable amount of travel, mostly to Washington D.C. His job, however, paid very well and allowed the family to afford a comfortable lifestyle in this upscale neighborhood of suburban Boston. Jennifer enjoyed her part-time job at the Wellesley Public Library that kept her busy three days a week and allowed her to pursue one of her passions—art history.

Bill was still getting himself organized upstairs as Jennifer finished her morning cup of coffee. *We don't have anything in the refrigerator. I should get over to Whole Foods early to beat the Saturday rush, and then I can spend the afternoon outdoors,* she said to herself.

She walked out to the garage and pressed the automatic garage door opener, only to find that Bill's Buick Century was parked on the driveway, blocking her Toyota Avalon. *I can't get out! He forgot to put his car in the garage last night. Should I just wait and go later? No... better to go now and get it over with.*

Jennifer stepped back into the kitchen and called up to her husband, "You've got me blocked in. Is it okay if I take your car to the store? I'll be back in about an hour."

"No problem," Bill responded. "Sorry about that. I'll be here. Just gonna have some breakfast and read the paper."

Jennifer peered into the mirror near the back entrance, put on some lipstick, and, using several quick strokes with a small brush, primped her short blonde hair. She scooped up Bill's car keys from the granite island in the kitchen and walked out to his car. She clicked the wireless access button on his key chain to open the front door and sat down behind the steering wheel. *Damn! My sunglasses are in my car.* She got out, walked back into the garage, and retrieved her sunglasses from the dashboard of the Avalon. *This is so typical. Just when I'm in a hurry. I should have made him move his damn car!*

She walked back to Bill's car and sat down again behind the steering wheel. She put the key into the ignition and turned it. Suddenly, a booming sound startled her. A powerful blast erupted from the hood of the car as a bomb exploded in the engine.

She screamed. The windshield shattered. Instinctively, she brought her hands up to protect her face, but it was too late. Shards of glass had already sprayed viciously into the car attacking her face and body with sharp debris. Intense, burning heat flashed over her as a second explosion erupted from the rear.

Smoke and fire engulfed the car. She let out another painful, agonized scream for several seconds, but then blacked out from the combination of the tremendous force of the explosion and the fire that rapidly spread through the cabin.

Bill heard the explosion and rushed downstairs. "Oh, my God! Jennifer! No!" he cried as he reached the burning car. He tried to open the door to help his wife but recoiled from the intensity of the heat and fire. He grabbed the door handle, burning his fingers, but it wouldn't open. He ran around to the other side, desperately trying to get in. But, it was no use. Helpless to save her alone, he ran back into the house and called 911.

"Emergency, 911. State your name," said the police dispatcher.

"There's been an explosion at 5 Kings Drive. My car blew up and my wife is in it!" Bill yelled into the phone.

"Try to stay calm, sir. Please state your name."

"William Clark. Get some help here right away!"

"Emergency vehicles are on their way. Can you give me any more information about this explosion? How many people are injured?" asked the dispatcher.

Bill offered no reply. He held the phone away from his ear, stared at it for a second, and then firmly placed it on the base. His heart pounded. Beads of sweat dripped from his face as his head hung down, and he leaned forward with his arms outstretched on the kitchen counter.

Tears welled up in his eyes. Bill knew it was too late. He had seen enough videos of car bombings from the Mideast to know that his wife was dead.

Chapter Two

The force of the explosion rocked the entire block, and the thick black smoke from the fire brought several neighbors running to the scene. They all looked bewildered, trying to fathom the incredible spectacle of a car bombing at a private home in this safe, suburban neighborhood. A fire truck, an ambulance, and two police cars with sirens screaming arrived within minutes. The firefighters doused the fire with a chemical spray that left the car smoldering on the driveway as a charred residue of metal and twisted plastic.

Burned beyond recognition, Jennifer Clark's charred body was removed from the car, wrapped in a series of white blankets, and placed into the ambulance. The emergency vehicle sped away while the small, but growing group of spectators looked on in disbelief. Bill Clark, numbed by the shocking event, stood on the lawn, off to the side of the destroyed car, receiving hugs and expressions of sympathy from neighbors who tried to console him. The acrid air reeked with the smell of smoke and burned human tissue.

A seemingly perplexed young police officer approached Bill and asked, "Mr. Clark, can you tell us what happened here?"

Bill struggled to regain his breath. "I don't know," he gasped. "I was upstairs and heard a loud noise. By the time I got down here, it was too late," he said. His voice choked on the last few words.

"Do you have any idea who could have done this?"

"No," he said, shaking his head slowly. He winced as his eyes watered from exposure to the smoke. "But, I work for the National Security Agency in the counterintelligence division. This could be a terrorist act."

The officer looked at Bill as if he'd suddenly realized things were even more complicated than he'd thought. He looked around, almost wondering what he should do next. Sensing his confusion, Bill continued, "I'll contact my home office in Washington. They'll have a crisis team here within a few hours."

The officer nodded and walked back toward the car, leaning in toward the smoldering chassis to get a better look at some fragments lying on the ground. "Don't touch anything," Bill warned him. "Forensics will need to analyze everything. Even the residue may tell us what device was used or give us a clue about who planted it."

As Bill watched, the police officers circled the car and placed yellow crime scene tape around his driveway. *These local cops have no clue what they are up against. A car bombing in Newton, Massachusetts, with international implications? They've never seen anything like this.*

Bill knew this was a case for the special investigators of the NSA and the Department of Defense. They would exhaust every possibility until they found the people who were responsible for this deadly act. *But now, I'll be under intense scrutiny not only from the people who tried to kill me, but also from those trying to protect me.*

For Bill Clark, despondent over the loss of his wife and suddenly nervous about his own safety, a detailed investigation into his private life was the last thing he needed.

Chapter Three

Ten days later in Fort Meade, Maryland, Bill sat in a conference room at the National Security Agency with eight investigators from the NSA and the Department of Defense. A broad-shouldered man of medium height, Bill wore a gray, pin-striped suit with a red tie. The fatty tissue of his neck draped over his buttoned shirt collar, betraying the fact that he needed to drop twenty pounds or buy a larger size. At first, the mood in the room was very sympathetic. Everyone expressed their sincere condolences about the tragedy that had befallen Jennifer Clark and asked how Bill and his two children were holding up in the face of such unexpected and heart-breaking circumstances.

"Luke and Marissa went back to school yesterday. They're kids with strong character. It will be tough for them, but they'll be all right once they get back into their school routine. They both have great college friends who will give them emotional support while they're away from home." Bill's demeanor wavered only when he mentioned the names of his children, and from then on, his voice was calm and controlled.

When Bill finished thanking everyone for their concern, the room became quiet for a few seconds. Then Dom Melone, the chief investigator for the Department of Defense, leaned forward on the oval conference room table and slid his reading glasses down a little farther on his nose so that he could look over the rims directly at Bill

Clark. Melone's words quickly changed the sympathetic feeling of the meeting to a tone that was strictly business.

"Bill, we've done an in-depth analysis of the explosives that were used on your car. It was a very sophisticated bomb rigged to the ignition system." Bill looked at him with a blank expression and nodded.

Melone continued. "They used wires from an electrical blasting cap to points along the ignition and stashed a fair amount of plastique into a hollow cavity behind the dashboard. That ensured that the full force of the explosion would be directed to the driver and passenger in the front seats. And, just to make sure that they didn't miss, there were other wires running back toward the fuel tank where we found residue of high-order explosives: mercury fulminate and ammonium nitrate. When they exploded, it set off a flash fire that engulfed the car almost immediately. There was no chance for anyone to escape from that car alive. This was not the work of amateurs."

Bill listened impassively to the details being presented to him. Melone's matter-of-fact description made him feel like he was attending a typical NSA inquiry about the death of a foreign agent in Europe or somewhere in South America. It was so depersonalized that he found himself dissecting the information as an investigator from the NSA rather than the widower of the car bomb's victim.

Gary Warrington, another investigator from the Department of Defense, was the next person to speak. "Bill, we think that you must have been followed for a while and that the individuals who did this were waiting for the right opportunity. Was it usual for you to leave your car on the driveway rather than parked in the garage?"

"No," said Bill, sensing that the real inquisition had officially begun. He nervously pushed a few stray hairs back from his forehead and twitched his neck muscles. "I always park the car in the garage. But when I got home that afternoon, Jennifer's fitness trainer had parked in front of my garage door, so I just left my car on Jennifer's side of the driveway figuring that I would move it later." Bill paused for a second, shrugged his shoulders and shook his head from side to side in order to convey the insignificance of his actions on the day before the tragedy. "We had dinner… I did some work in my office … we went to bed early. Forgot all about it until Jennifer called up to me the next morning from the kitchen."

Warrington, a tall, athletically built man who looked to be about thirty years of age, stretched back in his chair and continued speaking. He looked as though he was trying to appear nonchalant in his approach, but it didn't work. "Did you hear any noises during the night that, looking back on things, you might think were suspicious?" His tone was probing as if waiting for a slipup or incriminating misstatement.

"No, our bedroom is located upstairs on the far side of the house, away from the driveway. The kids are both away at school; their bedrooms look out onto the driveway. So I didn't hear anything. And if Jennifer heard something, she never mentioned it to me."

"Have there been any unusual encounters in the past few weeks? Something that didn't seem to fit with your normal routine?"

"No...nothing," replied Bill. His hands now rested comfortably on the table. Each measured response seemed to fortify his resolve.

"Was there a person or a car that seemed to recur in places that you frequent?" Warrington asked, continuing to test his subject.

Bill's response was quick and to the point. "Hey look, Gary, I've been with this agency for eighteen years. Like all of you, I'm trained to keep an eye out for things like that. This came out of the blue. Nothing tipped me off to make me think I was being followed or under any kind of surveillance," he barked.

"Just a second here, guys," said Melone as he held out his hand and interrupted the questioning before tempers flared. Bill shot a hard stare at Warrington who seemed unmoved by the emotional response and lightly tapped his pen on the conference room table.

Once again, Melone used his calm, deep voice to remind everyone to maintain their objectivity. "This appears to be the work of an Al-Qaeda operative who had help with the technological aspects of the bomb. We've seen a similar pattern in several car bombings in Europe. Al-Qaeda claimed credit for all of them. It most likely took two people working together to rig it in the middle of the night when no one would see them. I assume they were watching you for a while, waiting for the right opportunity. They probably intended this as a message to us. Sort of a 'We know who your agents are, and we can get to them' kind of message. The fact that this occurred outside of Washington is further support to that theory. Finding a department head from the

NSA in the Washington area is too easy. With this car bombing, they were making a statement for the whole world to see."

The room became silent as everyone digested Melone's theory. Then Melone took off his reading glasses and looked directly into Bill's eyes. "Bill, I know you've been through a lot, but I'd like you to meet with two of our agents for a day or so of debriefing. Are you up for that?"

"Of course. No problem," Bill said.

"Good. Any attempt on an agent's life has to be investigated to the fullest. We want to make sure we're not missing anything. We don't want any more surprises."

"I understand," said Bill.

In a conciliatory manner, Melone then asked, "Bill, when that part of the inquiry is finished, would you like to take a leave of absence for a couple of months? We know this must be a tough time for you."

Bill responded without hesitation. "No, I'd actually be better off if I got right back into the projects I was working on. We were in the process of straightening out a lot of algorithm issues in our cryptography division. If I stay home for a few months, I'll have too much time on my hands to revisit what happened. I've got to move on. Working will be good for me."

As he looked around the table at the eight faces staring at him, he could tell by the nods and slight smiles that his words had been accepted by a sympathetic audience. Bill had survived the first round of interrogation.

But he knew, from this day forward, he had to be careful every step of the way.

Chapter Four

Daniel Cormac Gallagher Jr. was surrounded by piles of papers and cardboard boxes. The sleeves of his blue, button-down-collared shirt were rolled up unevenly in a haphazard way. His trim, six-foot frame leaned forward with his elbows resting on his desk as he studied the contents of a manila folder. Gallagher had decided to close his Commercial Street office and get out of the business of being a private investigator. But he had never imagined this paperwork nightmare would be part of it. The files and reports he'd accumulated over the past seven years couldn't just be tossed in the trash. Some had to be archived in a safe place where they could easily be retrieved. Others needed to be shredded to protect his clients' privacy. His chore was to separate them into their proper category. *What a mess! I wasn't cut out for this tedious crap.*

Gallagher had spent the past few months finishing up a few lingering cases before closing his office for good. He had recently tracked a missing teenager from Billerica who had found her way to Brooklyn, New York, and was about to fall prey to the vagaries of street life. Her high-school friends had refused to give him any information. But he found one girl who blinked nervously when he asked if her friend had tried to contact her, and he convinced her to cooperate. She eventually provided the information he needed to locate the runaway and bring her home to her family.

Gallagher knew he would miss the satisfaction he remembered from these cases—along with the element of excitement and brain-teasing. He loved the challenge of putting the pieces together and solving the puzzle, even though there might have been considerable risks along the way. Gallagher also understood the pain of families who had lost a loved one and needed an answer. The death of his younger brother more than twenty years ago had been a powerful motivating factor in his career as a private investigator. Fighting the boredom of his new job in the business world would not be easy.

But it would all be worth it to ease Kate's mind. Two months ago on a glorious September afternoon in Brewster, Massachusetts, a small group of family and friends had gathered to watch him exchange wedding vows with her under a flower-covered archway framed by the setting sun over Cape Cod Bay.

Kate's smiling picture on his desk, showing her brown hair with auburn highlights and her beautiful hazel eyes, served as a pleasing reminder of his good fortune. Gallagher knew he had found a true soul mate—a woman with whom he could find happiness for the rest of his life. But the price of this happiness was steep.

After two nearly fatal encounters while he investigated a multiple murder and conspiracy case in West Castle, Massachusetts, Kate had made him promise to put away his gun and abandon his career as a private investigator. Reluctantly, he had agreed to pursue a new business: setting up security systems for large companies in Boston that were concerned with protecting their inventory as well as their customer files. This new venture could be profitable, but it would be a far cry from the intriguing and stimulating cases to which he had become accustomed. In his private moments, he tried to create a plan where he could keep Kate happy and continue with his career. So far, he had come up empty.

Now, however, he had to face up to the task of sifting through his old files. His personal secretary, Diane Beane, was still helping him and, as usual, kept him organized. In fact, he had hired Diane to work with him on his new project, knowing full well that he'd be lost without her.

Diane was busy emptying her desk in the outer office when the telephone rang. After a few minutes, she came into Gallagher's office and said, "Dan, there is a woman on the phone who would like to make an appointment."

"Great," he said.   "Did you tell her I'm going into early retirement?"

"Yes, I said that you weren't taking on any new cases, but she insists on at least talking to you."

"Just what I need to officially drive me out of the business—someone I don't even know, and she won't take 'no' for an answer."

Diane smiled, but continued with her plea.   "Even if you don't accept her case, she hopes you might be able to refer her to someone. She sounds pretty desperate. What would you like me to do?"

"Well, I'll be here for a few more hours going through all of these papers. If she doesn't mind sitting in the middle of a bunch of cardboard boxes, she can come over this afternoon. I can talk to her for a few minutes and see what she wants," he replied as he tossed a small folder toward an ever-growing pile near the paper shredder.

Diane left for a few minutes, then returned.   "She'll be here in about an hour."

"No problem," said Gallagher, hardly paying attention to the message as he continued tossing papers to the floor. His mind had shifted into cruise control, idly reviewing documents and trying to keep his thoughts from wandering too far astray. *I guess I'd better get used to referring these cases away; I'll be doing a lot of that from now on.*

Chapter Five

Gallagher shuffled through the papers on his desk. He leaned forward with his chin on his left hand, occasionally running the fingers of his right hand through his black hair. Distinct strands of gray had taken a prominent position, but the thickness of his hair helped it to stay in place with little combing. His concentration was interrupted by a light tap on the door. He looked up and saw Diane standing in his doorway with another woman. "Dan, this is Jeanne Campbell. She called earlier for an appointment."

"Please come in and excuse the mess. As Diane told you, we're in the process of closing the office," he said as he stood up and removed a stack of files from one of the chairs in front of his desk. "Have a seat and tell me how I can be of help to you."

Jeanne Campbell entered the room sat down in the chair. Gallagher made his usual five-seconds assessment: attractive—mid-forties— short blonde hair that looked natural rather than artificially colored— beautiful blue eyes highlighting her face. She wore a navy-blue pants suit that would easily be appropriate for an administrative position. Gallagher hesitated to guess her occupation, but had a feeling she gave orders rather than received them.

Gallagher sat behind his desk and cleared a box out of the way so he could look directly at his guest's face. "Give me a two-minute summary, and I'll see if I can refer you to a colleague who might be able to solve your problem," he said, opening the discussion without delay so he could get back to the work at hand.

His guest didn't disappoint him as she wasted no time getting right to the point. "My twin sister was Jennifer Clark. She was killed in a car bombing at her home in Newton three weeks ago." She paused for a few seconds to let the impact of her words register and then quickly asked, "Have you read about it in the newspapers or seen the stories on TV?"

Gallagher's eyes widened as he shook his head affirmatively and answered, "Yes. That was awful. I'm sorry for your loss. The reports said that it was a terrorist act directed at her husband. Doesn't he work for the CIA or NSA....one of the federal spy agencies?"

"Yes, Bill works for NSA. He is a cryptography analyst, and he's worked on counterintelligence projects for years. He's based in the Boston office but spends a good deal of time in Washington and the NSA main office in Maryland."

"I think I read that your sister decided to take his car in the morning, and then the car exploded?" asked Gallagher, trying to remember the details as he spoke.

"Yes, Bill's story is that he had inadvertently blocked Jennifer's car the night before. So she ended up taking his car when she wanted to go to the food store."

Gallagher quickly picked up on two of her words. "You said, 'Bill's story' with a hint of sarcasm. Does that mean you don't think he's telling the truth?"

"I don't know what to think. There are so many thoughts going through my mind. But something happened in the past week that made me believe there is more to my sister's death than the fact that she simply got into the wrong car one Saturday morning," she said.

Campbell had now garnered all of Gallagher's attention. He could feel the tingling excitement that always occurred when he was on the brink of hearing the framework of an unsolved mystery. He thought how much he would miss this feeling; nothing he could do in the business world would come close to replacing it. "What happened to give you that idea?" he asked.

"As twins, my sister and I shared things that no one else knew. I knew a secret about her life that no one in her family can ever know. She was having an affair…" she said.

A married woman having an affair was hardly earth-shattering information to a person in Gallagher's line of work, but he had to admit that the story became more interesting when she finished her sentence.

"… she was having an affair with another woman."

Gallagher waited for a few seconds to see if she volunteered any additional information. When she didn't, he asked, "Was this always her preference?"

"No, she was happily married for many years. Then, about two years ago, she began confiding to me that some changes had occurred; she could no longer suppress her inner feelings. It had happened gradually over a period of years, but she preferred women to men."

"Do you think this other woman put the bomb in her car?" he asked. "From what I read in the newspaper, that was a pretty high-tech explosive. Seems to me your brother-in-law's car must have been rigged by an expert, not an amateur."

"Yes, I know all of that. Let me tell you a little more about my sister's lover and you'll see why I have so many questions. Her name is Marcie Williams. Jennifer and I were taking a course on art history on Wednesday afternoons at the Museum of Fine Arts. Jennifer loved that subject. She could spend hours in the museum and never get tired of it. There were ten women in the class. Then one week, a new woman joined our group. It was Marcie. She and Jennifer hit it off right away; I could tell there was instant chemistry between them. Before I knew it, they were spending time together after class and on days when Bill was out of town. Jennifer confided to me that their relationship was more than just friendship. They had become lovers."

"Was Marcie also married?" asked Gallagher.

"Yes, but she said she and her husband had separated."

"How long did their affair go on?"

"About two and a half months. At first they would meet at a motel on Route 2, or if Bill was out of town, right at Jennifer's house in Newton."

"Why didn't they just go to Marcie's apartment? Wasn't she living alone?" Gallagher asked, already trying to ferret his way into the story.

"That's what I asked Jennifer myself. But she said that Marcie was afraid that too many people in the apartment complex knew her and she didn't want her personal tendencies known until her divorce was finalized. So, many of their rendezvous were at Jennifer's house while Bill was away."

"I'm still not seeing how all of this pertains to the car bombing," he said in the hope that additional facts would justify her concerns.

"After my sister's death, I tried to call Marcie to tell her what happened. I figured that my sister cared about her and would want her to know. But I couldn't reach her anywhere. Her cell phone number was disconnected. She had vacated her Cambridge apartment, and she never came to another class at the art museum. She just vanished," Jeanne said, shaking her head in disbelief at her last three words.

Gallagher pressed on with his questions, still not convinced of a link to the car-bombing incident. "Her disappearance, in itself, may not be that pertinent to what happened to your sister. Maybe something sudden and unexpected came up in Marcie's life and she had to deal with it?" he said.

"Maybe so. But her disappearance made me think back to a few things that Jennifer told me. Marcie always preferred to go back to the house rather than the motel. Said it was too expensive to keep renting a room for a few hours. One day, following one of their afternoon trysts, Jenn came out of the shower and found Marcie roaming around the house. She was in Bill's study, standing behind his desk. She asked what she was doing, but Marcie said she was just interested in how they decorated the house. Jennifer thought some of her actions were odd, but mostly, she just laughed them off. She was so smitten with her that I think she chose to ignore a lot of things."

Jeanne shook her head again, as if unsure of the significance of what she had said and still puzzled by the skein of facts she'd presented.

Now that he had a better understanding of her reasons for concern, Gallagher asked the inevitable question. "Do you think Marcie had some connection with the people that tried to kill your brother-in-law, Bill Clark?"

"I'm not sure, but I'm leaning that way. It seems like she was trying to get into the house when she knew Bill would not be there."

"You'd make a pretty good private detective. That's the same conclusion I reached a few minutes ago."

His compliment didn't seem to boost her spirits. She continued to look dismayed by the entire topic, as if the pain of losing her sister and presumably closest confidant could not be erased.

Gallagher sensed her uneasiness and tried to offer her some support. "Would you feel better if someone could find Marcie Williams and tell her about your sister?" he asked.

"Yes. I need to know if she was the wonderful person my sister talked about or a fraud with a hidden agenda. Mr. Gallagher, Jennifer actually told me that she was ready to tell Bill about the affair and ask him for a divorce. She loved this woman and was willing to give up her marriage to be with her. Her biggest fear was how her children would handle the news. I can understand how she felt. Under the circumstances now, I'd prefer that they never know about her affair."

"Well, that leads to another question. With your sister's sexual preferences, did they have any recent problems in their marriage? Do you think her husband had any suspicions about her involvement with another woman?" he asked, figuring that no question was out of bounds at this point.

"I've talked this over with my husband, Rich, and we agreed: They basically stayed together because of their children."

"A lot of couples do. But there must be more you could tell me about their relationship."

She sighed deeply. "Yes, there is. Jennifer always suspected that Bill was seeing another woman. In fact, she found a crumpled piece of paper in his study about six months ago. Part of an address was scribbled on it. Bill got angry when she asked about the address and refused to answer. It was a real confrontation. But he was involved in so much cloak-and-dagger government work that his trips and time away from home were always 'classified information.' With Bill, if he didn't want to discuss something, he would merely say it was 'off limits'—end of discussion. After enough years of that stuff, it's hard to keep a marriage from unraveling. As far as Bill's knowledge about Marcie, I don't think he knew. I guess we have to ask the question, though: If he did know, would he have done something to get rid of my sister?"

Her voice trailed off as she seemed to consider her own question and the serious ramifications that it brought to the discussion. Was this a matter of a clever husband doing away with his wife under the smokescreen of a terrorist incident? However, it was entirely too early to jump to any such conclusion.

"So you want someone to find Marcie Williams?" Gallagher asked. She nodded.

"I'll need a day or two to think this over," he said. "Maybe I can come up with someone who can take on this case for you. Give your contact information to Diane before you leave. I'll be in touch."

"Look, Mr. Gallagher—"

"You can drop the Mister," he interrupted with a reassuring smile.

The tense expression on her face relaxed. She smiled back and then slowly continued. "I know that investigations like this can take a lot of time and become expensive. I want to make it clear that I can afford your fee. I'm willing to pay whatever it costs to answer the questions about my sister's death."

With those final words, Jeanne Campbell stood up, reached out for Gallagher's hand, shook it firmly and walked out of his office. As she spoke to Diane in the outer office, Gallagher sat back in his chair, thinking about Jennifer Clark and the mysterious woman she had brought into her life. He assumed that high-ranking investigators from the NSA and the Defense Department were already working overtime trying to determine which terrorist group was responsible for the car bombing that was intended for Bill Clark but instead killed his wife.

However, it was possible that they were lacking a critical piece of information—a piece that could only be supplied by locating the suddenly missing Marcie Williams.

Gallagher could feel the undeniable forces drawing him back into the fray.

How could he convince Kate that he needed to investigate one more case?

Chapter Six

The waiter carefully placed the plate containing an appetizing arrangement of *escargot au beurre d'ail* in front of the single diner at a table for two in Le Cirque, one of the finest French restaurants in Las Vegas. It was only six o'clock in the evening—early for dinner in this electric city known for late nights, gambling, entertainment, and great food. Le Cirque, a five-diamond, award-winning restaurant, was generally included in the top-ten lists of the best dining establishments on the Strip. The restaurant overlooked the lake at the Bellagio Resort and was famous for its sweeping, multi-colored, silk-tent ceiling.

It was the kind of elegant atmosphere that Lan Tauber enjoyed when he decided to dine alone. There were times when he needed to reflect on his plans, gather his thoughts, and chart his future course of action. Tauber had an unofficial but powerful position in Las Vegas: Head of Special Operations for the major casinos.

The past year had been full of turmoil. He had been hounded by the FBI—repeatedly questioned about his role in the West Castle murder case, his relationship with the now-imprisoned former congressman William J. Prendergast, and his association with an unknown man named Jerry Murray. There were constant inquiries about Johnny Nicoletti, a hired hit man who was killed in Massachusetts during a foiled attempt on the life of a private investigator—a guy who knew

21

too much and kept sticking his nose into the business of the Las Vegas Syndicate—a thorn in his side named Daniel Cormac Gallagher Jr.

However, Tauber had managed to dodge all the attempts to link him with the murders and bring an indictment against him. No one had been able to prove that he knew the fictitious person, Jerry Murray. There was no proof that he had ever even spoken to Johnny Nicoletti. As far as his relationship to the congressman, he maintained that it was strictly a case of a Las Vegas lobbyist trying to present rational economic reasons why a bill before Congress should be defeated.

Looking away from his view of the dancing fountains in the lake, the exquisitely dressed man in his late sixties with a ruddy complexion and neatly combed white hair directed his attention to the appetizer in front of him. He tapped his fingers lightly on the table; his distinctive blue-sapphire ring glistened in the lights from the colorful ceiling. He had much to consider.

Tauber had to admit that he admired Congressman Prendergast for his tenacity against the federal prosecutors. He had never buckled and never confessed to any part in the murders of the three real-estate partners who had paid him for his help to reduce a federal loan obligation. He merely admitted that he had taken a bribe and accepted the four-year prison term to which he had been sentenced. With time off for good behavior, he would be eligible for parole in eighteen months. Prendergast had to pay a fine of almost a million dollars—nothing for a man who had amassed a huge fortune during his congressional career. Overall, not a bad deal.

Most importantly, Prendergast had never fingered Lan Tauber. He was offered all types of plea bargains, but he never wavered. For that, Tauber would be eternally grateful. He would be sure to find some way to reward the former congressman when he was freed from federal prison. In the meantime, Tauber's contacts in the underworld were making sure that Prendergast's prison experience was not too stressful. Tauber knew that a happy, comfortable inmate was less likely to capitulate to the Feds and try to cut a deal for himself.

Prendergast's decision to remain silent, however, had a very practical aspect to it. He knew the kind of person with whom he had been dealing. If he had implicated Lan Tauber in the West Castle murders and caused Tauber to be sent to prison for conspiracy to commit murder, Prendergast's life would be in jeopardy. Although he might have escaped a prison term for himself, Prendergast would have spent the rest of his life looking over his shoulder, wondering what payback was in store from a mob that never forgave a rat.

All of these thoughts brought Tauber to the subject of the person most responsible for his problems during the past year. Although he had never met him or seen his picture, Tauber had a mental image of Gallagher, the private investigator from Boston who occupied his mind for a good part of every day. No one else had ever stood in his way as this guy had; no one else had ever gotten the best of him or posed such a threat to his future. In Lan Tauber's world, you paid a price for being such a nemesis.

As he sat patiently in this gourmet restaurant waiting for the next course to be served, Lan Tauber was relaxed and composed. After all, he was a man who never wasted time being angry—he simply got even.

Chapter Seven

Gallagher pulled into the driveway of his Needham home at seven o'clock that night. He and Kate had moved to this two-bedroom ranch-style condominium in May, a few months before their wedding. After the horrific gun battle that had taken place in his previous condominium at BayView Towers in Boston, too many nightmarish memories haunted Kate, and she could not continue to live there.

Before putting the condo on the market, they had hired a painting and plastering crew to repair the damages caused by the stray bullets and splattered blood that stained some of the walls and floors. When the workers were finished, no trace remained of the bloody scene that had occurred the night that Johnny Nicoletti and his accomplice broke into the condo, held Kate hostage and attempted to assassinate Gallagher.

The realtor who handled the transaction never discussed the incident with any of the prospective buyers, figuring that they would hear about it on their own after they moved in. This did not sit entirely well with Gallagher, whose high sense of integrity demanded full disclosure on all business dealings. However, he did recover from any pangs of a guilty conscience when, despite a slowdown in the real-estate market, he realized a hefty profit of nearly $100,000 at the closing.

Gallagher would miss the beautiful view over the harbor and all of the events that accompanied it—the fireworks displays on the Fourth of July and New Year's Eve, the tall ships sailing into Boston Harbor, and, most of all, the peacefulness and serenity of the water.

Their home in Needham was a new condominium development with beautiful landscaping and many creature comforts, including an interactive lighting system and a hydro-massage whirlpool tub.   Kate was the co-owner of a placement service, and her business was thriving. She and her partner had carved out a very successful niche in the lucrative field of "head hunting" for high-tech companies located in Greater Boston. They had developed an excellent reputation for finding qualified, experienced executives for management and supervisory positions. Since Kate did most of the interviews, the success of the business was a tribute to her keen insight into how people related to their coworkers and her ability to recognize those qualities that are necessary for leadership roles.

Gallagher's new venture would require a significant capital investment in order to get established and then months before it would be profitable. The lucrative fees he collected as a private investigator had now dwindled to a mere trickle. He was fortunate that Kate's business paid such handsome rewards. For the first time in his adult life, Gallagher had to admit he was a kept man.

Since Kate had so many business meetings in the late afternoon and early evening, very little cooking took place in their new residence. Gallagher, himself, was useless in the kitchen and freely admitted to this deficiency. Tonight's dinner was a take-out specialty from the Cheesecake Factory—Chinese chicken salad: a blend of sliced, roasted chicken with pea pods, rice noodles, almonds, and Mandarin oranges, topped with a tangy plum dressing. One of their favorite dishes. They both professed they were famished from a long day of work and dug into their dinners with enthusiasm.

"How did everything go today? Still cleaning up your files?" asked Kate, hardly looking up from her plate.

"Yes. I feel like I'm buried in paperwork. But, Diane's been great. We're almost done," he said, wondering to himself how he would broach the next subject. After a few seconds he continued, "I may have one more case to finish up. A woman came by today and needs some help with something," he said.

"I thought your last case was that girl from Billerica," she responded quickly. "What kind of help does this new woman need?"

"Oh, it's just a missing person case. It won't take me too long," he said, trying to dismiss the importance of the job.

"Who's the woman who needs the help?"

"She is the sister of the woman killed in that car-bombing incident in Newton a few weeks ago."

Now with a decidedly worried tone, Kate looked up from her dinner. "Wasn't her husband a CIA agent or something? Didn't they suspect that terrorists were involved?"

He continued to downplay the significance of the event. "Yeah, that's what the newspapers reported," Gallagher replied.

"After all we went through last year, I thought you had agreed to give up these dangerous cases."

"I don't think it will be dangerous—"

She cut him off before he could make any more excuses. "Did you forget what happened? Those men broke in to the apartment, tied me up, and held a gun to my head. It was a miracle we weren't both killed!" She emphasized the last few words, letting Gallagher know she was agitated and annoyed.

He wanted to be sensitive to her fragile emotional state and tried to mollify the situation. "I just have to help her find a friend who's gone missing. It's a complicated story, but it won't take me long."

Now obviously angry, Kate exclaimed, "What's wrong with you? You won't be happy until I get called down to the morgue to identify your body on a slab!"

"Kate!" he pleaded. But, it was no use.

She put down her fork and placed her napkin on the table. Her eyes were misty, and she swallowed hard, looking as though she were trying to keep herself from crying. "Maybe I should think about whether I should have married you in the first place." She got up, went to the bedroom, and slammed the door.

Gallagher wanted to immediately follow her, but knew she needed time alone. He took only a few more bites of his salad. He had lost his appetite, knowing the stress he had caused her.

He stood by the window for a few minutes, looking over the deck toward the wooded area that extended past the lawn. He was torn by the debate that raged in his mind. The two greatest loves of his life—Kate and his job as a private investigator—had become mutually exclusive. There seemed to be no way that they could co-exist, but his selfish side prevailed and he wanted both.

He walked to the bedroom door and tried to open it. It was locked. He knocked several times, but she wouldn't answer. "Kate, we need to talk this out," he called through the door. No response.

He threw himself down on the couch, clicked on the television, and tried to find an escape from the anguish of their first real fight as a couple. He flipped the channels—CNN, the Celtics game, a movie on HBO. Nothing worked. Nothing else seemed to matter. He felt miserable.

He alternately paced the room and tried to watch television. After more than two hours, he found himself, once again, staring out of the window overlooking the deck.

Then his thoughts were unexpectedly interrupted by her arms coming around from behind him, under his arms, and hugging him firmly. She leaned her head on his back. "Don't you know how much I love you?" she asked softly. "I'd do anything for you. But when one of these cases comes along, you become consumed. It's like some powerful force takes over and you forget what's important."

He turned around and looked into her hazel eyes, still moist with tears. The sadness did little to detract from the striking appeal of her face. He never tired of looking at her, but she possessed much more than good looks. Her strong and passionate inner core and her determined commitment to improve their life together surfaced as her greatest quality. He could always count on Kate. He needed her to stay with him. He tried to rationalize his plans. "This won't take long. Three weeks … maybe four. Once I find her, I'll turn everything over to the feds and come home. Then we can start all over again."

She shook her head. "No, something about this frightens me. There is danger here. Can't you see it? A woman was killed. Whoever did it won't be happy when you come snooping around."

"I can handle it. Don't worry."

His plea wasn't convincing. She pushed a few inches further away to emphasize her next point.

"No. If you choose this life, don't expect me to share it with you. I can't go through another time when I'm afraid to walk into the house or open a door because some horrible person is waiting for you with a gun in his hand."

"Kate—," he tried.

"No," she insisted, as tears streamed down her cheeks. "Maybe you should stay here, and I'll move back with my parents until I find another place. We both have a lot of thinking to do," she said, now having resigned herself to a self-imposed exile.

"Is that what you really want?"

Kate paused for a few seconds and then began speaking again, almost in a whisper. "What I want is for you to promise me that you'll be safe ... that you won't put your life in danger again."

He rubbed her hands and arms tenderly, trying to ease her fears. He hoped she could feel the strength of his body as she leaned forward again and hugged him. Was the thought that she might leave him somehow making her want him now more than ever?

She pressed closer to him. They kissed deeply. He could feel her body coming alive in his arms. As she pulled him closer, he could feel the warmth of her flushed skin and hear the soft moan of her quickening arousal. He leaned down, lifted her up, and carried her into the bedroom.

Hardly touched, the two abandoned Chinese chicken salads remained abandoned to wilt on the dinner table.

Chapter Eight

Kate had been right—he couldn't resist. The thought of finding the mysterious lesbian lover of a woman killed in a car bombing was far too tantalizing for Gallagher to pass up.

The next morning, Gallagher agreed to take on the case and began his search for Marcie Williams. He had obtained a photograph from Jeanne Campbell that showed several members of the Wednesday-afternoon art history class in front of the Museum of Fine Arts in Boston. A woman with short-cropped, black hair and bangs extending low on her forehead stood next to Jennifer Clark. Jeanne identified her as Marcie. The other women in the picture were smiling, almost hamming it up for the camera. Marcie, however, was not smiling. She was staring straight ahead at the person taking the picture. Gallagher assumed that she would have preferred not to be in this picture but had no diplomatic way of avoiding it. Although the photograph was not a close-up, Gallagher could see that Marcie Williams was an attractive woman with a very good figure.

Using the list of pertinent information from Jeanne Campbell, he set out to start the investigation. His first stop was the Human Resources Department at Prudential Securities. Not to his surprise, he was informed that no one by the name of Marcie Williams had ever been employed by that company.

Next he drove out to Cambridge and turned off Massachusetts
Avenue onto Walden Street, where he approached an apartment
complex consisting of two large red-brick buildings. The entrance
bore a large sign, "Walden Park."

The guard at the security gate opened the door of the small booth.
"Yes, sir?" he asked.

Gallagher leaned out of his car and faced the guard. "Just checking
on the availability of a rental unit." A lie, of course. But how else
could he get past this guy?

The guard pointed to a sign on a door labeled "Office." "Park your
car in one of those spaces and check in with the building manager," he
directed. The gate opened, and Gallagher drove in.

He parked his car, walked into the office, and closed the door
behind him. Seated behind the desk, a woman with dark-rimmed
glasses was finishing a telephone call. She placed the handset on the
receiver and looked up at Gallagher, suspiciously eyeing the six-foot
tall stranger who had entered her domain. "Yes, how may I help you?"
she asked with a forced smile, as she removed her glasses and tilted her
head to the side.

"I'm a private investigator trying to locate a missing person. I
believe she may have lived here," replied Gallagher. He placed one
of his cards on the desk in front of her and continued with the basic
facts. "The woman's name is Marcie Williams. It's important that I
find her."

The woman put on her reading glasses to peruse the card. She then
slowly took off her glasses, placed them on the side of the desk, and
folded her hands in front of her. From the condescending look on her
face, Gallagher could sense that a scathing lecture was forthcoming.
"Certainly you must know that the privacy laws forbid us from
disclosing personal information about our tenants," she said with an
affected manner and an arrogant grin. "We can only do so with a court
order or subpoena from the police."

"I appreciate your concern for your tenants," he replied. "But, it's a
matter of great urgency that I speak to Ms. Williams."

However, his argument fell on deaf ears. "Sorry, Mr. Gallagher.
I'm not at liberty to give you any information. I have nothing further

to say. I suggest that you leave the premises before I call a security officer."

Gallagher held up his hands and took a step backward, mocking the perceived threat. "That won't be necessary. Thanks for your time," he said, smiling with what he hoped was a sarcastic grimace. He retreated toward the door, opened it, and walked across the threshold, but he leaned his head back into the office for a parting shot. "You've been a big help," he said and firmly pulled the door shut.

As he walked out toward his car, he looked across the parking lot and saw a man sweeping the walkway in front of one of the large high-rise buildings. Gallagher wasted no time approaching him. He was wearing navy blue pants and a light blue shirt labeled, "Walden Park Maintenance."

"Excuse me," he said in a low voice. "I'm trying to locate a woman that used to live here. It's important that I contact her. Have you ever seen the woman in this picture?" he asked, as he took the photograph out of his sport coat pocket and showed it to the man while pointing to the black-haired woman standing impassively on the left.

The man carefully examined the photograph, blinking steadily as he stared at the face in the picture. Then he slowly looked up at Gallagher. "Did you check with the lady in the office?" he asked.

"Yes, but she wasn't very helpful."

The man in the blue shirt looked around to make sure no one was within hearing distance.

"That bitch!" he said angrily, "she wouldn't give you the time of day. Just likes to bust my hump all day."

Gallagher smiled and nodded in agreement. "Yes, my friend, I've already had the pleasure of meeting her."

Then Gallagher took a step closer and pressed him, "What about the woman in the picture? Do you recognize her?"

The man paused for a few seconds and then responded, "Yeah, I know who it is. I know her very well."

His answer was followed by a longer pause, as his eyes darted nervously around the parking lot and across the walkway leading up to the entrance of the high-rise building. Gallagher understood this pause and the associated look that accompanied it. This was the reason why he always carried two twenty dollar bills folded together in his right pants pocket. The look said, "I know what you want, and you're going to have to pay me to get it."

One twenty dollar bill used to be enough, but inflation had pushed the price upwards over the years. You couldn't buy very much information for twenty bucks anymore. He reached into his pocket and slipped the two twenties into the right hand of the man who had now moved a little closer to keep anyone from seeing this silent transaction.

"Tell me about her, Dave," urged Gallagher, his attention drawn to the name embroidered on the man's blue shirt.

"Rented 22-C in Building #1 … one of the furnished units. Used to come and go quite a bit. I helped her with her bags a few times when she arrived from the airport and sometimes let her know when her rental car arrived."

"You mean she didn't live here all the time?"

"Right. She'd fly in for a few days at a time. Usually, she would get here on a Tuesday and then leave on Friday. She was never here on the weekends. Must have had some business to take care of in the area and then would go back home."

"You said you sometimes let her know when her rental car arrived. What was that all about?" Gallagher asked, his interest clearly piqued by these new revelations.

"She got here by cab … usually a Boston cabbie. So that tells me she was comin' in from the airport. Then, an hour or so later, the Enterprise people would arrive with her car. Always the same car, a silver Dodge Stratus. A couple of times they must have gotten here early and were waitin' for her to come down. So I pushed her intercom button to let her know they were here."

"Did you speak to Ms. Williams very much?"

"Nah, only the usual pleasantries. She was nice enough, but not one to chat very much. More or less kept to herself. But, man, she was a real good-looker …a very sexy lady. Somethin' about the way she walked made you notice. Know what I mean?"

Gallagher nodded and smiled weakly, as each little nugget contributed to the rapidly growing image of Marcie Williams that was forming in his mind.

However, he hardly had time to ponder this latest addition to the visage. Dave excitedly continued, "But, I don't think her name was Marcie Williams."

"What makes you say that?"

"I know she registered here in the rental office by that name, but the name on the airline tag on her luggage said 'Rebecca Johnson.' I even heard the guy from Enterprise call her 'Becky' one time."

"Do you happen to remember the airport code on the luggage tag?"

"Yeah, it was DCA. She was comin' in from Washington D.C.," replied Dave with a confident nod, impressed with himself for his display of airport knowledge.

"You're a pretty observant guy, Dave. Good work. Anything more you could tell me?"

"She left for the last time a few weeks ago. Haven't seen her since. Her apartment is vacant now, and I don't think she's comin' back."

Gallagher handed one of his cards to his friendly informant. "Stick this in your pocket, Dave, and give me a call if you think of anything else or if she shows up again. I'd like to talk to her myself." Gallagher ended their conversation and thanked him for his help. Within a few minutes, he drove out of the apartment complex.

The forty dollars had proven to be a worthy investment. Gallagher had started his day looking for Marcie Williams. Now a new identity had entered the puzzle.

Why would this woman have an assumed name? Why did she romance Jennifer Clark and then abruptly disappear? Did she have a secret agenda as Jeanne Campbell had suggested? Or was this merely a case of a passionate fling that ended on a tragic note?

Gallagher knew there was only one way to answer all of these nagging questions—he had to locate the mysterious woman named Rebecca Johnson.

Chapter Nine

The oval table was surrounded by a group of cryptography experts from the National Security Agency. Bill Clark loosened his necktie and hunched his broad shoulders as he leaned forward on the table. He listened intently while members of the group explained how the security of top-secret transmissions could be guaranteed.

Clark had more than eighteen years of experience with the NSA. He had earned his doctorate in mathematics from Stanford University and, as a married man with a young family to support, had come to Washington for a job interview with the government. Impressed by his academic credentials and communication skills, the NSA hired him.

The Information Age was about to be launched. The development of public-key cryptography and the RSA cipher had revolutionized the science of encrypting messages to ensure privacy and security. Mathematicians with Clark's brainpower were in demand by U.S. intelligence organizations that were seeking ways to safeguard secret transmissions to U.S. allies from being intercepted by hostile nations. Clark's superiors recognized early on that he was not only smart—he had a photographic memory. This served him well in the complex science of cryptography.

Over the years, the diligence to his job had resulted in several promotions. He now had the lucrative position of Chief of Information

Assurance. This gave him control over and access to the most sensitive information at the NSA.

At issue today was the protection of data related to the transfer of weapons and strategic arms to China. For the past few years, the massive United States trade deficit with China had been skyrocketing. The Chinese government had kept its currency, the yuan, tied to the value of the U.S. dollar. By undervaluing the yuan, Chinese businesses could sell goods in the United States inexpensively. This had created a huge imbalance as United States consumers purchased far more goods from China than they sold to the Chinese.

Under tremendous political pressure to resolve this trade imbalance, the Bush administration had quietly convinced the Chinese government to reform their monetary policies to ease the deficit. In return, the U.S. had offered to help the Chinese fortify their northeast borders with North Korea by shipping weapons and strategic arms to critical secret installations within China. Communications related to these transactions between the United States and China were protected by encrypted coded messages.

"How can we be sure that this code can't be busted?" asked Clark. "We wouldn't want the North Koreans to get their hands on this information."

One of the mathematicians spoke up. "We're dealing with enormous numbers here. No one has the ability of factoring such large numbers to compromise the code. There is no computer technology available now or in the foreseeable future that can do the computations necessary to break the code."

Clark looked at one of the other young men at the table and tried to put him on the spot. "What do you say? Is he right about this?"

The young man fidgeted for a second and then responded. "Mr. Clark, if the transmissions are intercepted, we are very confident that no one will be able to decipher them."

All around the table, heads nodded in agreement.

"So you're telling me that we can have an ongoing dialogue about defense matters with the Chinese government, and the North Koreans won't know what the hell we're talking about?" Clark said. The six men sitting around the table all smiled and nodded.

"Very good....excellent work," said Clark. "Now all we have to worry about is whether one of you decides to sell the code to the North Koreans."

The room erupted in laughter. Bill knew they thought it was a ridiculous proposition. Everyone in the room had been carefully screened and interviewed by the FBI and the Defense Department before being selected for this task. They had been subjected to extensive background checks. These men were painfully aware of the consequences involved if any of the information they possessed was ever shared with an unauthorized person, let alone a foreign government largely viewed as a hostile antagonist.

The cost of being caught?—public disgrace, huge fines and years of imprisonment. It was a much higher price than any of them was willing to pay.

As Bill Clark enjoyed the response to his little joke, he knew someone in that room was willing to take such a chance. Someone who had figured out a foolproof way to go undetected—someone with a photographic memory who was capable of carrying information out of the Agency without ever removing a single piece of paper.

Bill Clark had made his decision a year ago.

Now it was too late to turn back.

Chapter Ten

Gallagher knew all private investigators thrive on good contacts, knowing people who will provide valuable information when it is needed the most. A well-placed friend in the state's Registry of Motor Vehicles is not just a good contact; she can only be regarded as an absolute treasure.

Gallagher pressed "7" on the speed dial list of his cell phone and smiled when the familiar voice answered the call. "Phyllis Sax!" he said, "It's been a long time, honey. How are you doing?"

"Gallagher, you rascal! Where've you been? I haven't talked to you in ages," she said. "Hey, I heard you got married. Who's the lucky girl?"

"Her name is Kate. But, I'm the lucky one in this relationship. She's pretty special."

"Well, be sure to tell her that she broke a lot of hearts when she captured you."

He grinned. "I'd do that, but I might have to answer some uncomfortable questions."

"You're right about that," she laughed. "But I know you're not calling me for belated wedding wishes. What does my favorite private eye need today?"

"Phyllis, I need a favor," he started, but she interrupted him with an even louder laugh before he could finish his explanation.

"Who are you kidding?" she roared. "Every time you call me it's because you need a favor! If you weren't so handsome I'd hang up on you as soon as I heard your voice."

"Listen," he continued, "I need some help finding someone, but she's not in Massachusetts. I've got a name and think that she's somewhere in the general Washington D.C. area. I can also give you a description and an approximate age if that helps."

"Gallagher" she said with a sigh, "you are an insufferable devil. Haven't you heard that there are privacy laws in this country that don't allow us to give out that kind of information anymore?"

"Yes, but I thought those laws didn't apply to us, Phyllis. We go back a long way," he said.

"All right, all right," she surrendered. "Who are you looking for?"

"A woman named Rebecca Johnson."

"Johnson?" she needled. "You couldn't have asked me to find someone named 'Smith' to make it a little tougher? There must be a million Johnsons in Washington."

"Sorry, I know it's a pretty common name. She would be in her late thirties or early forties, about five feet four with black hair. That might help you to narrow it down a little," he offered.

"Do I dare ask you what this is all about?" she said, poking fun at her friend.

"You can ask, Phyllis, but you know I can't tell. Someday we can talk about it over a hot-fudge sundae, and I'll be the one buying."

"It's a deal, sweetie. I'll see what I can do and get back to you. Now stay out of trouble, Gallagher, you have a knack for finding it." He could picture the wide smile on her face as she clicked off the phone.

Becky Johnson ... Becky Johnson..., he thought to himself, already adopting the familiar form of her name. *Let's hope I get lucky and there are only a few dozen of them that match.*

Chapter Eleven

The drive out to Newton Highlands only took about twenty minutes from his Boston office. Gallagher had arranged with Jeanne Campbell to get into her sister's house at a time when Bill Clark worked out of town so he could look around. He was curious to know why Rebecca Johnson, also known as Marcie Williams, had been so interested in exploring the Clarks' home.

Jennifer Clark had given Jeanne a key and the burglar-alarm code to the house years ago. As a result, Gallagher didn't have to resort to any of his lock-picking skills to gain entry to the house; he just followed Jeanne as she unlocked the door and walked in.

The Clarks' home was a modest, two-story English Tudor home in a quiet neighborhood. The kitchen bore the evidence of a man who had recently lost his housekeeper and was struggling with his newly inherited cleanup responsibilities. The sink contained a small pile of dishes, and the coffee pot on the counter was unplugged but still had the residue of drying coffee on the glass bottom.

Despite her lingering suspicions about her brother-in-law's role in her sister's death and his involvement with another woman, Jeanne told Gallagher that she'd maintained a reasonable relationship with Bill Clark. She was very close to the children and kept in contact with them frequently while they were away at college. She would come over for a visit every once in a while to help Bill straighten up the place or to bring him a home-cooked meal. Thus, her car in the driveway or her presence in the house would not have been unusual to him or any of the neighbors.

Gallagher walked through the kitchen and into the family room that had a sectional couch facing a wide-screen plasma television. Looking all around at the floors, the walls, and the furniture without making any comment, he worked his way slowly down a hallway toward the study at the far end of the house.

A window on the center back wall of this room looked out into the yard. The study had a large dark-mahogany desk facing the wall on the left. It was flanked by a three-tiered bookcase system that extended from the floor to the ceiling. The desk had ample work surface for a computer monitor, keyboard, and telephone and plenty of space for papers and writing. Judging from the large stack of mail and papers scattered around on the desk, this was a heavily used area of the house.

Gallagher stood in the center of the room carefully surveying its contents. He moved the chair away and gradually crouched down to look under the desk. Bending his head upward, he arched his back so he could see the underneath surface of the desk. He stared at the wooden panel below the pencil drawer.

"What are you looking for?" asked Jeanne.

Gallagher's left hand extended out from under the desk as if he were making a "Stop" signal. Bringing his head out from underneath the desk, he lifted his index finger to his lips and widened his eyes, indicating to Jeanne that she should not utter another word. She took a step back toward the door, frightened by his actions. He climbed to his feet and quickly ushered her out of the room, down the hallway and through the kitchen.

Once outside, he whispered to her, "The room is bugged. Someone placed a high-tech eavesdropping device under the desk. Your brother-in-law is probably not aware that all of his conversations in that room are being monitored."

"Who would be doing that?" asked Jeanne with a startled look on her face.

"I'm not sure," said Gallagher. "But something tells me that your sister's elusive friend, who called herself Marcie Williams, knows all about it."

Chapter Twelve

The young woman glanced nervously at the small clock on the vanity as she sat in front of her bathroom mirror combing her hair. Five minutes to ten in the morning. Her guest would be arriving in a few minutes. The volume of the television in the nearby bedroom was turned up so she could hear the local news and the weather forecast for tomorrow. It was going to be another cold day in Sterling, this Northern Virginia suburb of Washington D.C.

She wore a black silk bathrobe and black slippers, but nothing else. This would be a special occasion of sorts—an opportunity to make up for lost time. She had not seen him for almost two months. Circumstances had forced them to cool down their meetings for a while until he sorted out a few matters. Now, there was little that stood in the way of spending the rest of their lives together.

As she continued to methodically comb her beautiful long brown hair, she thought of the nice life to which she had grown accustomed. Living in this plush one-bedroom apartment with all expenses paid; plenty of money for clothes; a new Infiniti G35 in her garage; the prospects of an even better lifestyle to come with vacations and travel abroad.

True, he was a bit older than she, but only by about fifteen years. Not very much by today's standards. For her, a young woman in her mid-thirties, the difference hardly mattered when one considered all of the benefits the future offered.

She had thought that she might have to wait until he figured out a way to force a divorce. That would have cost them a large portion of his apparently ample financial assets and possibly brought attention to their secret liaison and, worst of all, alienated his family. However, fate had been on their side. Now they just had to be patient for a few months until they could gradually announce their relationship.

She put down her hairbrush, walked through the bedroom, clicked off the television, and then sat quietly in the living room, reading the newest edition of *Cosmo* while she waited. Within a few minutes, she heard a key in the door and watched as the knob turned to open. She moved quickly to the entrance way, throwing her arms around the man just as the door closed behind him.

They kissed passionately—two people who had been thirsting for the feel of each other for weeks and now united again without any fear of discovery. He pushed her back against the wall and peeled off her bathrobe to expose her naked body. The excited, groping frenzy continued as she tugged at him steadily, unbuttoned his shirt, removed his belt, and pulled him toward the bedroom.

Bill Clark and his mistress would spend the rest of the day in bed.

Chapter Thirteen

Tony Macmillan's eyes lit up as he reached for the phone on his desk. The senior Democratic Party advisor and one of the most knowledgeable and well-connected people in Washington had not heard from his old college friend in several months.

"Well, if it isn't Boston's version of Sam Spade!" exclaimed Tony with a laugh.

"Not quite," replied Gallagher, but he couldn't resist smiling.

"Oh, you're just being modest again. I know all about your life as a private eye ... full of excitement and intrigue."

"Hardly."

"Look at me. I just have to deal with the back-stabbing Republicans down here. You actually have days when bad guys shoot real bullets at you."

"That was last year. Things have settled down. I'm back to the mundane job of finding missing people."

"That reminds me. You never told me how you managed to escape from the two guys who were pointing guns at you in your apartment. Must have been scary."

"I was lucky. Wouldn't have been able to pull it off without Kate. She knocked one of them off balance as he was just about to pull the trigger and gave me the time I needed. She was very brave throughout the whole ordeal."

"Ah, isn't it great to be married to a real-life Wonder Woman?"

"Yeah, I guess that's a good description. I'll be sure to tell her for you," he joked.

"Had any postcards from Congressman Prendergast lately?"

"Doubt that I'm on his mailing list."

"That slimy bastard! Glad he got sent up the river. But when you look at his sentence, he really got off pretty easy. A measly four years for bribery? Too bad they couldn't convict him as an accessory in the murders of those real-estate partners in Massachusetts. I'll bet he was in on that up to his ears."

"You don't have to convince me," Gallagher agreed.

"And the irony of it all is when he gets out of jail, he'll still have plenty of money to live like a king!"

"Don't remind me. I still have doubts about the way the FBI handled that whole case. Someone got away with murder ... the same person who sent Johnny Nicoletti to kill me."

"One of these days you'll figure it out."

"Maybe."

"So, what can I do for you today? Somehow, I don't think this is a courtesy call," Tony said.

"Looks like I'm coming down to D.C. again," said Gallagher.

"What's the occasion?"

"No occasion. I'm trying to find a missing woman."

"I'm not hiding her."

"Didn't think you were. Her name is Rebecca Johnson, alias Marcie Williams. Sound familiar?"

There was a pause on the phone. Gallagher could almost hear Tony racking his brain, sifting through the hundreds of people in Washington with whom he came in contact on a regular basis. Gallagher hoped for a break. Not this time. "No, neither name means a thing. Is she involved with the government?"

"Don't know. All I do know is that she had an affair with the wife of a cryptography analyst who works for the National Security Agency—a guy named Bill Clark."

Tony gleefully interrupted. "Wait a second. I knew this would be juicy, but really? ... the NSA? ... a lesbian affair? How do you find these cases? What did I tell you? Excitement and intrigue are your middle names!"

"Well, their relationship didn't have a very good outcome."

"How so?" asked Tony.

"The wife was killed in a car-bombing incident."

"No!" Tony said. "I never expected that. Holy shit, Gallagher! I didn't think you were involved with another murder case."

"Sad, but true. And Rebecca Johnson disappeared right afterward."

"Ah, ha! a very suspicious move. See…this private eye stuff isn't so hard after all. Even I'm onto her. Why aren't the police looking for Ms. Johnson?"

"They don't know about her. The dead woman's twin sister hired me. The affair was secret. The husband and children didn't know anything about it either. Her sister prefers to keep it that way for the time being."

"The twin doesn't really think this woman set the car bomb, does she?" Tony sounded skeptical.

"We don't know what to think. All we know for sure is that Rebecca Johnson vanished and left a lot of questions unanswered. I'd like to find her and see just how much she does know about that car bombing."

Tony sighed. "Wish I could help, but those two names, Rebecca Johnson and Marcie Williams, don't sound familiar."

"What about the husband, Bill Clark? Ever run into him?"

"NSA is a big place. We don't have much to do with that agency. I never heard his name before, but I'll quietly check around and see what I come up with."

"Thanks, Tony. When I'm in Washington, I'll give you a call."

"Sounds good to me. I'll be here."

"We'll meet for dinner or a drink."

"Wait a second," said Tony. "Who's buying?"

"You never change," Gallagher said.

"Neither do you," Tony said. Then he laughed as he clicked off the phone.

Chapter Fourteen

The flight attendants on American Airlines #4599 from Boston to Washington D.C. pushed the beverage cart down the aisle and greeted the passengers with the usual requests for drink orders. Gallagher hardly noticed them. He was completely focused on the yellow notepad in his hands with a list of six women who shared two things in common—they all lived in the Washington D.C. area and were named Rebecca Johnson.

Phyllis Sax had given the information to him last night, and he had wasted no time booking this flight in the morning. Now, the difficult part would be to determine which one of the women used the alias Marcie Williams when she befriended Jennifer Clark. Gallagher hoped the addresses Phyllis provided were single-family residences rather than large apartment buildings. As they entered or left their homes, he could compare each woman's appearance to the picture of Marcie Williams that he carried in his pocket. He had looked at that picture so often that the image had become indelibly inscribed in his mind. He knew he would recognize her immediately.

An apartment building with many units, however, would make the task much more difficult. The thought of camping outside the front door while dozens of people came in and out did not appeal to him in the least. No, this would require a little bit of Irish luck—something he had learned to rely upon in his years as a private investigator.

After checking in at the Hotel Washington and reviewing a street map of the area, Gallagher drove his rented car to the first address on the list. It didn't take long to eliminate this Rebecca Johnson from his search. The woman who answered the door acknowledged that she was Ms. Johnson, but she was five foot ten with long blonde hair. And, she had no interest in purchasing the home security system that Gallagher pretended to be selling.

The second address was indeed an apartment building, so Gallagher moved on to another possibility on his list—1227 19th Street NW—the right side of a duplex home in a very nice neighborhood known as Dupont Circle. He rang the doorbell, but no one answered. Since the time was approaching six-thirty in the evening, he decided to sit in his car for a while in case the inhabitants would soon arrive home for dinner.

Waiting. Something you got used to as a private eye. Sometimes it could take hours before a break would occur; at other times, the hours of waiting were a total waste of time. But this happened to be Gallagher's lucky day. Only fifteen minutes later, a metallic black Acura sedan turned the corner and parked on the other side of the street, a few doors down from the duplex.

A woman emerged from the car. She shifted her small briefcase to her left hand as she closed the door and clicked her remote keyless system to lock the car. She wore a pair of khaki slacks and a waist-length, black leather jacket. Despite the darkness of the early evening, the light from the streetlight provided enough illumination for Gallagher to instantly identify the woman. Her short-cropped black hair with bangs extending down on her forehead were unmistakable—it was Rebecca Johnson, the woman known to the ill-fated Jennifer Clark as her lover, Marcie Williams.

Rebecca walked up the short staircase to the front door on the right side of the duplex and stopped briefly to remove the mail from the mailbox. She paused for a few seconds as she glanced through the envelopes, then turned, unlocked the door, and walked into the apartment.

Gallagher remained in his car contemplating his next move. He resisted the urge to go right up to the door, ring the doorbell, and force a confrontation. No, this discovery would pay its greatest rewards if he exercised a little patience. He needed to follow this woman and learn more about her. Where did she work? Who were her associates? Was she a foreign agent? The answers to these questions would help to reveal her role, if any, in Jennifer Clark's death.

Investigators from the FBI and the Defense Department had spent weeks trying to solve this case. To this point, they had no leads, no witnesses, and no plausible theories.

But Gallagher knew he was about to uncover the real story.

Chapter Fifteen

It might have been the result of too many cups of coffee or maybe the dozens of questions that kept rolling through his mind. Whatever the cause, Gallagher hardly slept that night. *I've got to cut down on coffee. The caffeine is killing me,* he thought to himself. It was, however, a hollow resolution—how else could he stay awake when he was used to sleeping so late in the morning? The wake-up call from the hotel operator had been at an ungodly time—five in the morning. But was there any other way he could be camped outside Rebecca Johnson's duplex early enough to follow her when she left for work?

"This better be worth it," he moaned as he tried to shake the grogginess out of his head.

There had been an interesting development the previous evening, just before Gallagher left Dupont Circle to return to his hotel. A man wearing a business suit and carrying a briefcase had walked down 19th Street NW and up the stairs to the same duplex unit as Rebecca Johnson. He had also paused at the mailbox, but the door to the apartment opened within a few seconds and Rebecca greeted him upon his arrival at home. The couple had smiled, kissed briefly at the doorway, and then closed the door behind them.

The exchange had been innocuous—like any other couple that had come home for a dinner together after a day at work. The pause at the mailbox was an indication that this man also lived in the apartment.

What other reason would he have to check for mail? But, who was he? Her husband? The man from whom she had claimed to be separated when she pretended to be Marcie Williams? Or was he someone new on the scene? Did he have any knowledge of her activities in Boston? Could he be an accomplice?

Gallagher usually did not make assumptions or jump to conclusions based solely on appearances. But he was fairly confident about one thing: This man, with a dark suit, white shirt, and tie, had the distinct appearance of an attorney from a corporate law firm. Those guys had a certain look that Gallagher found unmistakable.

For now, however, there were too many other questions to be answered, and he needed time to sort them all out. As he sat in his car at six-fifteen in the morning, sipping coffee, and struggling to keep his eyes open, the door to the apartment opened. The man, wearing a different dark suit but a similar white shirt and tie, emerged and walked down the street in the same direction from which he had come the previous evening.

Gallagher had scouted the area and knew the Metrobus line was located just a few blocks away. He assumed that the man was taking public transportation to downtown Washington D.C. He could not, however, follow him to confirm his theory; today, his attention would be completely devoted to Rebecca Johnson.

Two hours passed—the apartment door never opened. Out of coffee, having heard the morning traffic reports for the twentieth time, and fighting the urge to doze off for a while, Gallagher began to fear that she may have decided to skip work and sleep in. He tapped his fingers nervously on the steering wheel, resisting the temptation he felt last night when he almost rang the doorbell.

His perseverance was finally rewarded. At approximately eight thirty the door opened, and Rebecca Johnson walked down the short set of steps to the street. She was dressed in the same "business-chic" style with neatly tailored black pants and her black leather jacket. Her stride was fast paced and confident as she walked down the street toward her car.

Within a few minutes, her black Acura sedan was traveling southwest out of Dupont Circle. Gallagher made a quick U-turn with his rental and followed her at a comfortable distance to avoid being detected but close enough that he wouldn't lose sight of her car in the morning rush-hour traffic.

Okay, Ms. Johnson…. Let's see what you're all about, he said to himself as he darted in and out of lanes trying to make sure that he didn't get stuck at a traffic light, all the while keeping the Acura within two or three car lengths.

The trip took him down New Hampshire Avenue and then across the Potomac River and over the Theodore Roosevelt Bridge. After they crossed the bridge, Gallagher continued following the black car in a northwesterly direction on Memorial Parkway until it exited in Langley, a community that is part of McLean, Virginia. The distance was approximately eight miles and had taken only thirty minutes. Rebecca's car pulled into a secured parking area adjacent to a large complex of buildings that resembled a college campus.

Knowing that he could not attempt to enter the security-controlled parking lot, Gallagher continued driving for a few hundred yards and then turned around to observe the scene behind him. The complex of buildings included two six-story office towers, constructed of steel and glass, that were connected by a four-story core to another older-appearing concrete building. Above the main entrance, a sign read "George Bush Center for Intelligence."

Gallagher leaned back and considered the ramifications of his latest discovery: Rebecca Johnson, the mysterious woman and lesbian lover of the ill-fated Jennifer Clark, was employed by the CIA.

Chapter Sixteen

Gallagher could only conclude that Rebecca Johnson's daily routine was pretty boring. For two days, he had monitored virtually every move Rebecca Johnson made when she was outside of CIA headquarters. Each day had been the same: leave the apartment in Dupont Circle about eight-thirty in the morning; arrive at work at approximately nine o'clock; out for lunch to a local diner at noon; and then drive home for dinner at five o'clock. She had lunch with a man and two other women on one of the days, and ate alone on the other.

There was nothing remarkable about any of her actions. Gallagher knew he would have to talk to her in order to learn anything more about her relationship with Jennifer Clark and the possibility of her involvement with the car-bombing incident.

After she left CIA headquarters on the third day, she drove into Washington D.C. across the Potomac River, but then, instead of going back toward Dupont Circle, she headed east on Constitution Avenue, passing many of the historic government buildings—the Justice Department, the National Archives, the Museum of Natural History, and the National Gallery of Art. At Louisiana Avenue, she turned north and drove into the parking garage at Union Station. Gallagher had kept up with her all the way but had to back off for a few seconds as she entered the parking garage.

He caught a glimpse of her as she walked from her car toward the elevator. He parked his car and hustled toward the elevator, noticing as he got there that the cab had made stops on both levels of the main concourse. *That's just great! This place has more than a hundred shops and restaurants.*

He got off at the main concourse and walked around the huge, commercially redeveloped train station with its impressive barrel-vaulted, glass-paneled ceiling. He stopped occasionally and leaned against one of the large white pillars, hoping to spot his suddenly elusive target amidst the hundreds of shoppers bustling by. He looked in the windows of several coffee shops and boutiques but no sign of her anywhere.

After about twenty minutes, he went into the Station Grill, a restaurant with an old-time bar that had warm hardwood floors and a tin ceiling. The combination of textures yielded an inviting Victorian atmosphere. Gallagher loved the look of the place and took a seat at the end of the bar.

Hardly settled on his bar stool, he was jolted by the view directly across from him. A woman sat at the bar rather nonchalantly, with a cigarette in her left hand. Her chin pointed upward as she slowly blew smoke at the ceiling. Gallagher immediately recognized her—Rebecca Johnson.

The photograph he carried in his pocket hardly did her justice. She was much better looking in person. More importantly, he was instantly aware of the sensuous and sultry aura that she exuded. If he could only use one word to describe her, it would be "sizzling."

Perhaps it was the knowledge of her torrid affair with a woman. Or that she now lived with a man. Whatever the reason, he couldn't escape the feeling that sex was a high priority in her life. He found himself mentally undressing her.

Hey, what are you doing? You're still a married man, and you're supposed to be conducting an investigation into a murder! His own admonishment shook him back to reality.

She took an occasional sip from her drink, followed by a long, slow drag from her cigarette while purposefully looking around the restaurant and glancing at the other patrons at the bar. She never made eye contact with Gallagher, but somehow he knew that she was fully aware of his presence.

He ordered a drink and waited for a while, not saying anything but staring across at her until their eyes finally met. "Too bad about the smoking ban that's coming in January. Where will we go for a cigarette and a drink?" he offered.

There was no reply; she just took another long drag and looked away, as if completely repelled by his overture. The two men sitting between them were called for their table and smirked at Gallagher as they got up from the bar. If they had spoken, it would have been something like, "You'll have to do a lot better than that, buddy."

Gallagher moved a few seats closer so that now only one seat separated him from Rebecca who continued to coolly ignore him. "You come to this place often?" he asked, trying once again to innocently initiate some conversation.

"You should know ... you've been following me for three days."

She had clearly bagged him. No further need for charades. Now he was the one undressed. He raised his glass of Scotch to make a mock toast, "My compliments, Madame. I was trying to be discreet."

"You need more practice. I hope you don't do this for a living."

"In fact, I do. That's why I've been following you," he replied.

"Are you a cop?"

"No. I'm in business for myself."

"Oh, a private dick. Why are you following me, Mr. Gumshoe?"

"I've been trying to find a missing woman."

"Do you think I know her?"

"Yes, I'm sure of it."

"How can you be so sure? What's her name?" she asked, almost scoffing at his implication.

"Marcie Williams," he said dryly, knowing that he had played his trump card and should now take control of this verbal sparring match.

Rebecca put down her glass and nervously twisted her half-smoked cigarette into the ash tray. She looked away, swallowed hard and then stared coldly into Gallagher's dark brown eyes, "Yes, dear Marcie ... we do need to talk about her. But somewhere else; it's so unladylike to discuss such private matters at a bar."

Gallagher took her suggestion and walked over to the hostess. "We'd like a corner booth for two. How long is the wait?"

The young woman looked to the back of the restaurant and picked up two menus from her stand. "Follow me. I can seat you right now."

They followed the hostess on a meandering path that took them past crowded tables occupied by noisy patrons engaged in loud conversation. She stopped at a dimly lit booth against the rear wall and placed two menus on the table. "Enjoy your dinner," she said as she left the now awkward-appearing couple to decide which side of the table was preferable. Gallagher seized the initiative and motioned to Rebecca to take the left seat of the booth.

She glanced anxiously around the restaurant, as if to verify that no one was watching. Her hands fidgeted around her mouth—a sign that she could benefit from another cigarette, but she knew smoking was prohibited in the dining area. "I could be talked into another drink, Mr. Gumshoe," she said, apparently trying to reestablish her tough image and calm her nerves.

"Sure, what'll it be?"

"Ketel One on the rocks." Her voice was deep and seductive; it went along with the rest of her.

Gallagher motioned to a passing waitress who stopped in her tracks and came right to the booth. "Ketel One on the rocks for the lady; Dewar's on the rocks with a splash of club soda for me. And, bring a small glass of club soda on the side."

Now, with the introductory banter behind them, he looked cheerfully across the table at his antagonist and waited for her to speak again. She had been staring pensively at him, trying to size up this stranger who had suddenly come on the scene and obviously knew much more about her than she preferred.

Finally, the silence was broken. "What's your name?" she asked.

"Gallagher."

"Just Gallagher?" she mocked.

"Yes, when it comes to names, I'm into word economy. How about you?"

She ignored his smugness, still hoping to determine his motives without giving away any more information than was necessary. "Where are you from Gallagher?"

"Boston."

"I figured as much. Why are you looking for Marcie?"

"She had a lesbian lover who met a tragic end one morning when she put a key into the wrong car. My client thinks Marcie might know something about it. Seems that Marcie mysteriously disappeared right after the car blew up."

The waitress returned with the cocktails and placed them on the table. Rebecca took a sizable drink of vodka and let it slide slowly down her throat—the act of a person hoping for rapid absorption of the alcohol. She looked like someone seeking a better defense mechanism through a bit of lightheadedness. She paused for a while, looking away from Gallagher and then finally stared back into his unwavering eyes.

"Marcie Williams had nothing to do with Jennifer Clark's murder," she said coldly, stating the name of the victim for the first time, thus acknowledging her own assumed name.

"Why should I believe that?"

"Look, you're getting into a place where you don't belong. This is a complicated government matter. It involves classified information and dangerous foreign agents. You're in way over your head if you pursue this."

"I'll take my chances."

She kept pushing. "Guys like you end up with a bullet in their back when they ask too many questions. My advice is that you take your clever one-liners back to Boston and tell your client that you never found Marcie Williams. Let her name just fade away. Let it become irrelevant. "

"Sorry, I don't scare easily."

She looked around the restaurant again as if searching for the right answer while simultaneously assuring herself that no one was listening to their conversation. She took another sizable sip from her drink but said nothing.

Gallagher sensed her discomfort but pressed on. "The guy you live with …is he … uh … your husband?"

"No. We'll be engaged soon."

"What does he do?"

"He's a lawyer with a downtown corporate firm."

Gallagher silently congratulated himself for once again sizing up one of these guys by his stereotypical appearance. But he quickly got over his self-indulgence and continued with a question guaranteed to bring forth a reaction. "Does he know you're bisexual?"

Wham! Her palm slammed on the table, almost startling him. "You son of a bitch! Why don't you just go home and stay out of this before you get hurt!" she started to yell, but seemed to catch herself in the midst of her outburst, and she lowered her voice to a fierce whisper by the end of the question, as if she feared drawing further attention to their table. She looked rattled and upset but fully aware that she was facing a formidable challenger.

Gallagher's retort was firm. He held his hand forward, counting off on his fingers as he dramatized his points. "I've got a client in Boston who wants some answers. I'm going to get them one way or another. Do you think the *Boston Herald* would be interested in a story about Jennifer Clark's secret lesbian affair with a CIA agent who vanished right after her death? Sounds like front-page material to me. Somehow, Becky, I don't think your future fiancé wants to read about this in the newspaper."

He wasn't going away easily; she should know she couldn't scare him off with idle threats. Her demeanor changed almost instantly, like a poker player looking down at the opponent's winning hand and knowing her bluff had failed. She appeared to relax and breathe more easily as she leaned back in the booth, signaling it was time to surrender. The last remnants of vodka were consumed, and she waved off the waitress who offered to replenish her supply.

"Okay …let's agree to leave him out of this. Where should we begin?" she sighed.

"Why did Marcie Williams become part of Jennifer Clark's life? What were you after?"

"You have to understand: there's a lot I can't get into that's highly classified information. But, basically, the CIA was asked to look into leaks at NSA. Something was going on over there. They were getting sloppy about the way they handled encrypted messages involving national security. Our foreign sources were telling us that classified information was getting into the wrong hands. The Department of Defense investigators and the OIG couldn't find anything …"

"OIG?" interrupted Gallagher.

"Office of the Inspector General. Bunch of idiots. Couldn't find a leak if it was gushing at them. So the White House told us to get on it. We started checking NSA personnel who could be the source of the leaks. Bill Clark was on the short list."

"So you needed a way to get into his house and to plant that listening device under his desk?" asked Gallagher, providing further proof that he knew quite a bit about the surreptitious activities of Marcie Williams.

Rebecca lifted an eyebrow and wrinkled the right side of her lips as if to say "touché." Then she said, "You're no slug, Gallagher. You know a lot. But remember, even a little knowledge can be dangerous if the wrong people know you've got it."

"I can take care of myself."

"I'm not worried about you. I just don't want you causing me any problems," she said coyly as a slight smile crossed her face.

"Tell me more about what I need to know, and perhaps I can move on."

She continued with her story. "The Agency sent me to Boston. The plan was for me to get to know his wife. Meet her through an art class, befriend her, and eventually get into the house."

She paused as her voice trailed off, tears welled up in her eyes, and she bit softly on her lower lip, betraying an obvious crack in the tough exterior front. "What happened after that was something I never expected."

Gallagher waited for a few seconds, but she had become too emotional to talk. Then he filled in the blanks with the obvious continuation of her thought, "You had an affair with Jennifer Clark."

Her eyes were still moist, but she took a deep breath and gathered herself enough to continue speaking. "When I met her, there was an instant attraction between us. I don't know how else to explain it, but it was electric. I had no information going in to this assignment that she was a lesbian. No one at the Agency gave me a hint that she had anything but a happy marriage with Bill. I had always felt some of these tendencies myself, but managed to dismiss them—to keep them in the background. With Jennifer, I couldn't resist any longer. I figured I was in a different city with a new identity. No one knew me, and I would pull a disappearing act within a few months. So, why not? It was a chance to delve into new territory and test the limits of my fantasies. In the process, I could find out a lot about myself: who I was and what pleased me the most. As far as Jennifer was concerned, I represented the same opportunity for her. We cared about each other, but it was more of a convenient escape into a secret, experimental fantasyland."

"And then the car blew up," Gallagher added.

"Yes … that came out of nowhere. It shocked me when I saw it on the news. I contacted the Agency, but I knew right away that Bill had been the target. I wanted to call her sister and tell her I was sorry, but I couldn't risk it. Besides, no one at the Agency knew anything about my relationship with Jennifer. And, for many reasons, I wanted to keep it that way. I stayed in Washington and never went back to Boston. Marcie Williams officially ceased to exist."

"So who ordered the hit on Bill Clark?"

"No one knows. There's so much undercover stuff in these matters. If he was selling information, he could have been the target of counterintelligence operatives who would want to eliminate him. Another scenario says that the country he was helping had gotten all they needed from him and wanted to destroy the only witness that could cause them international embarrassment. Or maybe it's as simple as someone he stiffed on a gambling loan. Eventually we'll know, but so far it's still anybody's guess."

"Meanwhile, Bill Clark is still working for NSA," he said.

"Yes, and there's no proof that he did anything wrong. Three agencies have been monitoring this guy for the past three months and nothing has implicated him in any crime."

"What about his mistress?"

"Mistress?" she asked with a perplexed look.

"Come on, Becky. Jennifer's sister has suspected it all along. My guess is that Bill Clark wouldn't be the first member of the intelligence community to cheat on his wife."

"You're right about that. But if it's true, he's probably just trying to keep it quiet for a while until he decides to tell his kids. So far, we've found nothing to indicate he's been running around."

Rebecca's hostile attitude began to subside. He hoped something about him would make her feel that he was a trustworthy person, someone she could rely on to protect her secret private life, stop probing any further and go back to Boston. "So, tell me Gallagher, now that you've found Marcie Williams, what's your next move?"

"I'd still like to help my client find out who killed Jennifer Clark. Do you think Bill could have booby-trapped the car to get rid of his wife? Maybe his mistress wanted him all to herself and gave him an ultimatum? Think about it. He could have driven home that day and hooked up the explosives while she was asleep. I would guess it's a pretty fast job if you know what you're doing. Then he just stood back and let the government investigators pursue their crazy theories about Al-Qaeda."

"Anything's possible, but I doubt it. There's not one shred of evidence that involves him in Jennifer's death."

"Maybe you haven't looked deeply enough?"

"We checked his credit card purchases and sales of the explosive materials found in the remnants of the car. Nothing matched. Furthermore, nothing in his background would lead us to believe he had any knowledge or connections that could help him rig a bomb like that."

He looked down at the table and frowned. Then his gaze lifted away toward the ceiling as if he were processing another theory.

She studied him carefully as she slowly stirred the ice cubes that remained in her glass. Sensing that he was about to reply, she preempted him with another jab. "Give it up, Gallagher. That skeptical, private-detective mind of yours is a bit out of control. You're reaching, and you don't have the facts to support your theories."

"Hey, you like to test the limits of fantasyland," he fired back. "I like to test the limits of the real world. Sometimes the results can be very surprising. But maybe we can agree on something else ..." He paused for a few seconds.

She jumped in with encouragement. "I'm open to suggestions."

"I'm going to do some checking on Bill Clark and follow up on a hunch. If I find anything that helps your investigation, you can take it from there. Don't worry, I won't try to get involved in CIA business. I'll leave the dangerous stuff to you. In the meantime, I'll inform my client that Marcie Williams had nothing to do with Jennifer Clark's death. Marcie just prefers to stay off the front page of the newspapers."

"Consider this a friendly warning, Gallagher. You'd be a lot better off if you stayed completely out of this. You don't know what you're getting into."

"Sorry. I'm a big boy, and I can take care of myself. I just need a few more answers for my client before I let this go. As I said, I'll let you handle the 'spy versus spy' conspiracies."

What started as a testy confrontation had ended on almost amicable terms. They exchanged contact information and left the restaurant. Gallagher walked her to the black Acura in the parking lot and said goodnight. His pursuit of Rebecca Johnson had uncovered the story of Jennifer Clark's mysterious lover. Gallagher could only base his opinion on instincts, but he believed that Rebecca Johnson was telling the truth.

But, what about Bill Clark?

Something made Gallagher think Bill Clark had a lot to hide.

Chapter Seventeen

The phone at the Pine Hills in Plymouth, Massachusetts, rang four times before it was picked up. "Hey, Dad, hope I'm not catching you at a bad time," said Gallagher.

"Not at all. Your mother and I already finished dinner. I was just sitting here doing a little reading ... and some thinking." There was a distinct sadness in his tone. Unmistakable. Gallagher recognized it almost immediately. His thoughts flashed back to a day almost twenty-four years ago. A day filled with vivid images of excitement and then tragedy—a day he could never forget.

In his senior year at Boston College, Gallagher was a relief pitcher on the varsity baseball team. He was a very good pitcher, but not a great one, although like every varsity ballplayer, he had dreams of some day pitching in the major leagues.

The team had traveled to Florida in early March for their annual Southern swing, the highlight of which was the spring training exhibition game against the Boston Red Sox. The BC coach called him into the game in the sixth inning. Two men on; nobody out. This would be a challenging test, and Gallagher relished the opportunity. He loved the competition. He felt his heart racing as the coach handed the ball to him, walked off the mound, and headed toward the dugout.

Gallagher retired the first two batters—a pop out then a grounder to the first baseman. He was feeling good about himself. But, with two strikes on the next hitter, he threw a fastball over the middle of the plate. *Not one of my best pitches, for sure.* The ball exploded off the bat. Gallagher turned and watched the ball sail over the left field fence. A four-hundred foot home run. So much for whimsical dreams of the big leagues.

The excitement of the experience lingered for hours. He called his parents at home in Massachusetts. Despite the outcome, his father had been thrilled that he had pitched against the Red Sox. It didn't matter that he had given up a home run.

The team gathered in several of the hotel rooms and partied until well after midnight. Celebrating a loss? Of course, they had lost. A lop-sided score in favor of the professionals. But the college kids had met and played against some of baseball's biggest stars. In one afternoon baseball game, they had collected enough memories to last a lifetime.

For Gallagher, however, the excitement was short-lived. Just after three o'clock in the morning, a knock on the door of his hotel room awakened him. His coach stood in the hallway. The poor man seemed lost for words. Something terrible had happened. Gallagher's younger brother, Tommy, a sixteen-year-old junior in high school, had been critically injured in a serious automobile accident. It had been a stormy night with wet, slippery roads. Another teenager had been the driver, who was killed on impact. The coach had made arrangements for Gallagher to return to Massachusetts on an early-morning flight. By the time Gallagher got home, Tommy was dead also.

It was a time of unspeakable sadness for the entire family. His parents never recovered from the grief of losing a child. Gallagher despaired at the loss of his only brother. It affected him in many ways. Totally distracted, he barely got through his final semester of college. Playing baseball, once a great part of his college life, now seemed trivial. He never pitched for his team again. As a witness to the personal devastation of his parents, Gallagher developed an understanding of the emotional pain a parent suffers when a child is lost. This provided him with a deeply-rooted motivational drive in his eventual career as a private investigator; he never gave up on a case involving a runaway or a missing child. He became consumed with his cases, relentlessly pursuing leads until he reached a resolution. The parents of these kids needed answers; he always tried to provide them.

"Are you okay, Dad?" he asked, bringing himself back to the present.

"Well, you know, this time of the year around Tommy's birthday is always tough." Even now, more than twenty years later, his father would drift off into idle thoughts, wondering how the accident could have been prevented. *Why did we let him go out with his friend, an inexperienced driver, when the forecast called for heavy rains?*

"I know, Dad. It's tough for all of us. It's been a long time, but it still hurts."

"Are you in town?" his father asked.

"No. I'm actually in Washington."

"Oh, is Kate with you?" he asked, as his voice perked up.

"No, I'm alone. She's staying with her folks in Brewster for a while."

"Really? Is there some problem?"

Gallagher hesitated for a second. "No ... no problems."

"You two aren't getting a separation, are you?"

The time wasn't right to go over the issues in his marriage. "No, it's nothing like that at all. She's just staying there until I finish up with a case I'm working on."

"Well maybe there's a message for you. Enough with the cops-and-robbers stuff. Isn't it time to settle down to a business with a little less danger? Didn't you get enough of that last year?"

Gallagher could sense that the lecture was about to begin. He knew how his parents felt; they had lost one son, they didn't want to lose another. "I'm working on that, Dad. It will be sooner than you think. But, for now, I could use some help from a certain history expert I know."

His father was a retired history teacher at the Rivers School in Weston, Massachusetts. Despite his retirement, he still devoured the contents of three newspapers every day and read numerous books and periodicals to keep current with the political landscape throughout the world. Gallagher had never met anyone who could match his father's knowledge and clear perspective of world events.

"Okay, but I charge by the hour when a private detective calls," he joked, now showing signs of rebounding from his sad ruminations. "What is it you need to know?"

Gallagher explained that he was working on a case in which a government official was suspected of selling secrets to a foreign country. "I'd like to get a better profile of this guy and understand his motives. I need to know the likely source of the money."

"Oh, that's a tough call. Historically, there have been many governments willing to pay for top secret information about us. But if you look at the world as it is today, we're at peace with the Russians and the Chinese. Germany and Japan are our allies. Since 9/11 we've been consumed with the wars in Afghanistan and Iraq. None of the tribal factions we're fighting there have the wherewithal to bribe any of our officials. They just rely on terrorism."

Gallagher had opened the spigot and the information kept pouring out. His father continued, "I just recently read an article taken from *The Washington Post* that discussed the findings of the Senate Select Committee on Intelligence. They are reviewing evidence on nuclear, chemical, and biological programs suspected in Iran and North Korea. There is considerable proof that North Korea supplied uranium hexafluoride to Pakistan."

"Uranium hexafluoride? Sounds like dangerous stuff."

"Yes ... it's a substance that can be enriched to weapons-grade uranium. Very dangerous stuff. Pakistan, supposedly one of our allies, then sold it to Libya, certainly a country you'd have to categorize as one of our enemies and a country we don't want to be armed with nuclear weapons."

"So, you mentioned Pakistan, Libya, Iran, and North Korea. Who is the most likely candidate to be paying for information?"

"North Korea ... absolutely. They have the natural resources in minerals and raw materials that can upset the balance of world power. And they seem to have plenty of money up there."

"How's that? Thought they were an impoverished country."

"That's true of the general population. But the government regime has tons of money, mostly gained illegally. There are stories that they were even counterfeiting U.S. hundred dollar bills and then using the money to build up their nuclear arsenal. So if they wanted to bribe someone to get some top-secret information, they certainly have the money to do it."

Gallagher continued the conversation with his father for several more minutes, but stopped short of providing any further details of the case he was investigating. He mentioned nothing about the woman who was killed in a car-bombing incident or her link to a CIA operative. Too much danger and intrigue for family members. No need to conjure up more fears and worries.

"Dad, I'll give you a call when I get home. I want to come down to see you and Mom."

"Sounds good to me," his father replied.

"And thanks for all the information. This really helps."

"No problem. Just be careful. Something tells me there's more to this than you're willing to let on."

"Don't worry. Everything's fine."

He said good night to his father and clicked off the phone.

With every bit of information he gathered, Gallagher inched closer to the truth about Bill Clark.

Chapter Eighteen

The message on Tony Macmillan's answering machine had certainly piqued his interest: "Meet me at the Old Ebbitt Grill tomorrow at one o'clock and tell me everything you know about North Korea."

Tony had been expecting a call from his old college friend, but had to admit the subject matter surprised him.

North Korea? What could Gallagher be involved with this time?

"What's the deal here? Have you abandoned the private-detective business for a shot at international diplomacy?" ribbed Tony as Gallagher took a seat across from him at the restaurant.

"You know me, Tony; I like to constantly expand my horizons."

A waiter arrived and poured the coffee. Tony took a sip and flashed a big smile through his blonde handlebar mustache that was populated by more than a few gray hairs. They had been friends for years, and much of the joy in their friendship was based on poking fun at each other. Tony didn't miss this opportunity. "Expand your horizons? Are you kidding? A year ago we had lunch in this place and I gave you some help. Then, before I knew it, you were trying to save your ass while ducking bullets on a highway up in New Hampshire. And if that wasn't bad enough, they went after you in your apartment in Boston! Now you want to get involved with the North Koreans? How good are you at dodging nuclear weapons?"

"Hey, I'm not planning a trip over there. I'd just like to know how someone might try to get secret information to the North Koreans."

"Oh, that's even better. You're planning an act of treason! I think I need a little background information here before I become an accomplice."

Gallagher began with the latest updates to their last telephone conversation. First, he fired a mini-rocket. "Well, I found Rebecca Johnson."

Tony's eyes widened and he lightly stroked the right side of his mustache with his index finger. "Ah yes, the mysterious missing lover," he said, as if salivating for more specifics.

Then Gallagher dropped the bombshell. "She works for the CIA."

"Whoa! Getting juicier all the time," Tony said excitedly. He wiggled to the edge of his seat and leaned closer. "Tell me more."

"They were spying on Bill Clark because they thought he could be selling information on secret codes to a foreign government."

"The cryptography analyst?"

"Yes."

"Do they have the goods on this guy?"

"So far, the investigators have come up dry."

"Not surprising. These spies are pretty clever. Some of the famous cases involving treasonous counterintelligence agents took years before they were caught."

"Right."

"What about the car bombing? Who do they think was responsible?"

"The prevailing theory is that it was a terrorist act targeting Bill Clark."

"Sounds like you're not buying that theory," said Tony flatly.

"I don't know, Tony. If three government agencies can't find any evidence that this guy is selling secrets, I wonder if he just threw everyone off track and came up with a clever scheme to get rid of his wife. While everyone is looking into complicated international scenarios, he could have hired some techno-weirdo to rig a bomb in his car."

"But why did his wife's lover skip town after the car bombing?"

"Just didn't want to explain the affair. Their personal relationship was an unexpected sidelight to her assignment to spy on Bill Clark. She had nothing to do with Jennifer Clark's death. She was as shocked as everyone."

"She didn't by any chance, uh ...," Tony fumbled, motioning upward with his hands, looking up to the ceiling, pretending to search for the right words, "in any of her discussions with you happen to give you any, uh, specifics about their intimate activities?"

"No, you dirty old man, nothing you need to know," Gallagher retorted. Then, he flashed a sheepish grin. "But I wouldn't share them with you anyway. It's all part of client-investigator confidentiality."

"You're a cruel friend, Gallagher," Tony said. "You know how I live for these vicarious tidbits."

Gallagher laughed, enjoying his friend's act. Tony sipped more coffee and gradually recovered. He took off his rimless glasses. As he cleaned the lenses on his napkin, he looked quizzically across the table. "But, tell me, why the interest in North Korea?"

"From what I recently learned from a famous history professor, it seems like the logical place to start."

Tony nodded a few times and smiled. "Sounds like your dad has been prepping you for this case," he said.

"You're right. But, I need to know a few more facts so I can begin to sort out Clark's options and understand what motives he could have had in all of this."

Tony shifted into serious mode. "For starters, have you heard of the Doomsday Clock?"

"Yes; what's the relevance to North Korea?"

"Well, as a reminder of the dangers of nuclear proliferation, the *Bulletin of Atomic Scientists* recently moved the Doomsday Clock to seven minutes before midnight. That's the closest it's been for a long time."

"Why is that?"

"All because of North Korea, a sleeping monster waiting to attack. It's ruled with an iron fist by Kim Jong-Il, who's long been suspected of stock-piling nuclear and biological weapons and selling them to terrorist groups. To make matters worse, the capital city of Pyongyang has a bunch of Chinese criminal gangs that have smuggled counterfeit

U.S. currency and drugs into the United States. We've imposed financial sanctions on one of their main banks in Macao, near Hong Kong, where we believe the money laundering took place."

Gallagher listened intently, thinking of how many hours in the library his recent conversation with his father and this informational lunch were saving him. Tony continued to explain how other Asian banks had joined with the United States to boycott transactions with North Korea, setting off an unofficial financial embargo against the renegade country.

"South Korea has even put pressure on them by suspending rice and fertilizer shipments to North Korea. There are millions of people starving up there, and the government spends most of its resources on building an arsenal of nuclear weapons. Food distribution is controlled by the government, and members of the Workers Party and those loyal to the regime are given preference. A lot of young children and elderly people go without food," explained Tony.

"You mean they just let them starve to death?"

"In many cases, yes. There are some humanitarian efforts, such as the UN World Food Program. The North Koreans let them bring food and medical supplies across the border, but their activities are closely monitored, and they never let the volunteers anywhere near the nuclear facilities or prisoner camps."

"Is that the only way westerners can get into the country?" Gallagher asked.

"Yeah, that's just about it. Their border security is very strict. They're taught to shoot first and ask questions later. It's almost impossible for us to get information out of there. It's like a big, black hole in our intelligence operation."

"If someone was going to try to get rich selling information to them, what kind of secrets would they want?"

Tony spread some garlic butter on a roll and took a bite. He alternated his jaw movements between chewing and talking. "Well, you can see why they're so pissed off at us. We caught them red-handed with the money laundering and counterfeit currency. They'd like nothing more than to stay one step ahead of us by decoding our messages to foreign governments, especially the Chinese."

"Why the Chinese?"

"The North Koreans are very much afraid of China and would love to know where their military installations are located. And we've been helping the Chinese with their defense capability ever since they devalued their currency and helped Bush with the trade deficit. The North Koreans know we've become friends with China, and they don't like it one bit."

"What's the relationship of the NSA, the OIG, the Defense Department, and the CIA? Seems like they should be working together to find out where these information leaks are coming from," Gallagher pointed out.

"That will never happen. They're like squabbling little kids: jealous of each other and always pointing fingers to make the others look bad. It's entirely possible that there are no leaks. This could all be a result of the collective paranoia of our intelligence community. Maybe the car blew up because that NSA analyst owed some bookie a ton of money and refused to pay it. You should have learned that lesson from your last case when those guys from Las Vegas went to extremes and tried to bump you off. Sometimes, it's all about money."

Tony was now the second person to suggest that Bill Clark may have welched on a debt to the wrong guy. *Could it all be that simple?*

They ordered lunch and sat together for almost another hour, as Tony continued to provide a comprehensive review of the issues the United States faced with North Korea. Gallagher felt as though he had just attended a graduate seminar on international relations.

As the waiter cleared the dishes away and they reviewed the dessert menu, Tony changed the topic and asked, "By the way, what's Kate doing while you're messing around down here in Washington?"

"We agreed to live apart until I'm finished with this case. After all she went through with that West Castle case, I understand how she feels."

"Sounds serious. Are you two going to be all right?" asked Tony.

Gallagher avoided a direct response. "She's staying with her parents at the Cape for a while." He paused for a few seconds and then continued. "This is my last job as a private eye, Tony. I promised her I'd take up the more sedentary life as a businessman."

Tony laughed, "That'll be the day! This kind of stuff is in your blood, my friend; you won't be giving it up so fast."

Gallagher took another sip of coffee and smiled, wondering if his old college buddy had even more insight than he thought.

Chapter Nineteen

The drive to Sterling, Virginia, was less than forty miles and took just about an hour. Gallagher felt compelled to play out his hunch for at least one more day before returning to Boston. He considered this little jaunt a minor scouting mission. He had obtained part of an address, "Devonshire Unit 4-B, 20165," from Jeanne Campbell, who was proving to be an excellent deputy detective. It was the address her sister had found months ago, scribbled on a piece of crumpled paper in the waste basket of Bill's study. Jeanne had saved it; he wasn't sure why. But, at that time, her sister, Jennifer, seemed to be the loyal wife to a cheating scum bag. If they divorced, a paper trail to his extra-marital affairs could prove invaluable.

But what about today's excursion? A wild goose chase? Perhaps meaningless? Both of the above. However, worth the stretch if it provided some answers to the questions about Bill Clark's life.

One thought had left Gallagher feeling uneasy after his meeting with Rebecca Johnson: Why was Bill Clark's involvement with another woman of such little significance to the CIA? Money and sex always seemed to be the prime motivators in crimes. Why was the second factor being ignored? Why was Rebecca so reluctant to talk about it?

"Turn Right on Idle Brook Terrace," said the woman's voice of the GPS system from the dashboard console. Gallagher dutifully obeyed and found himself in the midst of a beautifully landscaped area that surrounded the handsome exterior of the Village on Potomac Shores, a luxury apartment complex in this quaint Northern Virginia town.

Gallagher parked his car and walked around for a while. Twenty minutes before noon on Sunday. From the visitors' parking area he looked across at the Devonshire Building. He tried to think of a believable sham story that would work if he rang the doorbell. Nothing clicked, but as it turned out, he was glad it didn't. While his mind was drawing a total blank, the door to Unit 4-B opened and a husky man with light brown hair appeared in the doorway. It was Bill Clark. Bill walked out to the driveway toward his car. *Good thing I didn't rush up there and ring the doorbell. I might have blown my cover.*

A dark-haired woman waved to Clark and quickly closed the door. Gallagher would have loved to get a better look at her, but at best, her appearance had been a fleeting cameo.

Bill got into his car and drove away. He had neither a suitcase nor a travel bag. Was he leaving for the apartment he maintained near the NSA Headquarters in Fort Meade? Or perhaps just running an errand and then coming back to spend more time with his love interest?

Gallagher followed him. It was not easy to avoid being detected since it was a Sunday morning with very little traffic on the roads. He stayed far behind hoping not to lose sight of Clark as he turned on several winding roads. The destination, however, was only a few minutes away.

Just after crossing Algonkian Parkway, Bill pulled his car into a large parking lot in front of Our Lady of the Snows Catholic Church. He was dressed in a blue blazer with gray slacks and an open-collar shirt. Gallagher watched as he walked into the church along with dozens of parishioners who had arrived for the Mass at noon. After a few minutes, Gallagher entered the church and sat in a pew on the right side near the back entrance.

The church was not fully occupied so he had a clear view of Bill Clark sitting on the left aisle about ten rows in front of him. The shrill sound of bells announced the arrival of the celebrant priest and almost startled Gallagher who was deep in thought, studying every move made by the man in the blue blazer.

There was, however, nothing to observe. Bill Clark participated in all aspects of the Mass—kneeling and praying at the appropriate times as if this were his usual Sunday practice. When the ushers passed the collection basket during the Offertory, he placed his donation in the basket. He offered the sign of peace to those sitting near him by shaking hands and stating the words, "Peace be with you."

Gallagher watched him carefully, but observed no signals or acknowledgments that could vaguely be construed as a clandestine effort to convey a message to someone in the church.   Clark sat motionless as the priest delivered his sermon, a short but passionate plea for Catholics to continue supporting charitable causes throughout the world.

After the homily, Clark received communion from the priest, returned to his pew, and bowed his head in prayer. At the end of the Mass, he left the church without speaking to any of the parishioners and drove back, as Gallagher predicted, to the apartment complex at the Village on Potomac Shores.

The whole exercise had been curious, to say the least. Had this man, suspected of treasonous crimes and cheating on his wife, suddenly found solace in religion? Could he have been involved in his wife's murder? Was his attendance at church merely a ploy to create the illusion of a religious man—an upstanding member of the community? But why here, far from his home where no one appeared to know him? And what about the new woman in his life? How much did she know about her lover's possible illegal activities? Many questions, but few answers.

Within a few hours Gallagher was on board a US Airways flight returning to Boston. He tried to put these issues aside and concentrate on his meeting tomorrow with Jeanne Campbell. She had hired him for one purpose only—to find Marcie Williams. He had accomplished this goal. Now he planned to inform her of the facts he knew to be true, that Marcie Williams had nothing to do with her sister's death. Furthermore, the police, the CIA, and investigators from the Department of Defense had found no evidence that implicated her brother-in-law, Bill Clark, in any crime, including the car bombing in which her sister had died.

Gallagher was running out of ideas, and it looked like his hunch on Bill Clark may have been completely wrong.

Chapter Twenty

It was hardly the type of gourmet establishment Lan Tauber usually chose for a luncheon meeting. But on the visitor's side of the main concourse of the General Mitchell International Airport in Milwaukee, Wisconsin, the choices for fine dining were rather limited.

He had selected this restaurant because of its location outside the security clearance gate. It was also a busy place where travelers grabbed a quick bite or a drink before their flight. The rapid turnover of customers offered the anonymity he desired—to sit at a table in the back of a restaurant in an airport he had never visited in a place where no one knew him.

For Lan Tauber, today's meeting would be a chance for retribution and to begin the process of settling an old score and reconcile a personal balance sheet that had unexpectedly tipped against him. His appointment was scheduled for two o'clock, but his guests were already twenty minutes late. He waited at his table impatiently, keeping a close eye on the entrance and watching for two men who would peruse the restaurant looking for their contact, who was a man they had never met and whose name they did not know. Their instructions had been simple: Meet at General Mitchell's Cafe at two o'clock in the afternoon and look for a man with white hair and a charcoal-grey sport coat.

About fifteen minutes later, a tall man walked into the restaurant. He had thinning brown hair and wore jeans and a short-sleeved, light blue denim shirt. He glanced around, surveying the tables one by one, until his gaze reached the lone diner in the rear section. They made eye contact. The tall man made his way back to the table and sat down.

"You're alone?" asked Tauber.

"No, my partner's at the bar; just wanted to make sure we had the right guy and weren't walking into a setup."

"Very good. I like doing business with guys who are careful."

The tall man turned and raised his hand, signaling toward the bar where another man promptly put down his drink and joined them at the table. The second man had a thick, brown, wiry mustache, a goatee, and a shaved head. He was not that much shorter than his partner, but his width was impressive. Although his body type might be classified as broad and muscular, the fact that his protruding gut stretched his tight tee shirt and hung over his jeans made Tauber think that only a few beers separated him from obesity. However, his bulky, stove-pipe arms looked powerful and served as clear deterrents to anyone who would be foolish enough to challenge him.

"My name's Lou Wilson, and this is Ben Harris," the taller man said as he nodded toward the expressionless person now seated at the table.

"Nice to meet you," replied Tauber. "You followed my instructions about getting here?"

"Yeah. We took a cab from downtown."

"Good. I don't want the license plate from your car to show up on the airport parking records."

Wilson ignored the repetition of over-zealous precautions. "Your name?" he asked.

"You don't need to know my name; you only need to know what I want."

"And what is it you want?" Harris chimed in with an edge of sarcasm in his voice.

"To eliminate a problem."

"That's usually an expensive request," said Wilson.

"Yes, I know the overhead for these jobs runs pretty high, but no one pays as well as I do." The debonair older gentleman spoke smoothly, displaying his confidence and experience in handling such serious negotiations.

"Who's the mark?" Wilson asked impatiently.

"A private eye in Boston."

"Why him?"

"He took something away from me about a year ago."

"What'd he take?"

"He killed one of my best men."

"So now it's payback time," Wilson said and nodded knowingly.

"You could call it that if you like. I consider it more along the lines of re-establishing the proper order of an imperfect world. Some of us have no tolerance for losing," said Tauber.

"Winning is expensive. Are you prepared to pay for your little victory?" asked Wilson, clearly the vocal leader of the tandem.

Tauber opened his sport coat and took a white envelope from the inside pocket. He slid it across the table toward the two men. "Ten thousand now … twenty thousand more when the job is done. His information is in the envelope with the down payment."

Using his thumb in the manner a poker player would inspect the hole cards, Ben lifted the flap of the envelope slightly to check the contents. He slowly fanned the neat stack of one-hundred dollar bills. His firm nod to Wilson confirmed that the money count appeared to be correct.

"One more thing …" added Tauber. "His wife was partly responsible for my loss. I won't be disappointed if she becomes a casualty. Uh, what's the phrase they use now? Collateral damage?"

"Shouldn't be a problem. But, an extra hit means …" started Wilson, but Tauber interrupted him before he could finish his proposal.

"… an extra ten thousand," said Tauber. He flashed a broad, tight-lipped knowing smile.

"How do we collect the balance?" asked Ben, breaking his silence and seemingly tantalized at the thought of a bigger payday.

"Same as today. We meet here when the job is done. Get the word to your contact in Chicago. I'll be in touch with him."

"How can we be sure you'll show?" asked Ben, clearly the skeptic of the two.

"Let's look at the flip side. How can I be sure you won't take my ten thousand and screw? You see, boys, life is built on trust. And who knows? This could be the first of many lucrative gigs for both of you."

The two hit men smiled as Lou shoved the envelope into the front pocket of his jeans, a clear indication that a deal had been struck. With the business portion of the meeting concluded, they ordered lunch and a round of drinks, like three old buddies who just happened to meet at the airport.

Nothing was signed, but Tauber knew they had consummated a binding contract nonetheless—a simple, but deadly transaction intended to end the lives of Mr. and Mrs. Daniel Cormac Gallagher Jr.

Chapter Twenty-One

The look of anticipation on Jeanne Campbell's face signaled the nervous tension she was trying to contain. Missing her twin sister and her best friend, Jeanne had thought of nothing else for weeks. Sitting across from Gallagher in his office, she was about to learn the identity of the mysterious woman who had vanished after her sister's death.

"I was able to track down Marcie Williams," he started, wasting no time with unnecessary preliminaries. "In fact, I had quite a long conversation with her."

"And....?"

"She works for the CIA, and she was sent to Boston as part of an investigation into your brother-in-law's activities with NSA. He and a number of other counterintelligence agents have come under scrutiny."

"Bill? For what?"

"Someone's been selling secrets to a foreign government and the CIA was trying to find out who's responsible for the leaks. Her assignment was to get close to Bill without him knowing it ... to get into the house and plant a listening device so they could monitor his contacts."

"So that's how the bug got planted in Bill's study."

"Right. Her relationship with your sister was an unexpected byproduct of all of this. She had nothing to do with Jennifer's death."

"So everything about her was a lie?"

"That's how they operate."

"And what's she doing now? Just moving on with her life like nothing ever happened?" she said as her voice became emotional. Her lips quivered, and her eyes filled with tears.

"It's a cold business. But she told me they've looked into all possibilities and, at this point, they haven't been able to produce any evidence that links Bill to the car bombing. And they have no proof that he is involved in the selling of information to a foreign country."

"That figures. No one has a clue," she said. Her voice trembled and she bit her lower lip.

Gallagher sensed that she was on the verge of breaking down and tried to offer some consolation. "The case is still under investigation. Hopefully, they'll have some answers for you soon. For the time being, Bill continues with his job at NSA and is free to do whatever he wants."

"I suppose that Marcie Williams was not her real name."

"No, it was a fabrication, like everything else you and your sister were told. But I do believe she had true feelings for your sister. Only the two of them really know what might have happened to their relationship had she not been killed."

"Will she talk to me?"

"No, I think she prefers to go on with her work and the privacy of her life. Frankly, I don't see any benefit to a meeting with her. I know it's painful, but you have to begin to seek some closure with this."

"It's not fair," she said as a large tear trickled down her face. "Everyone just moves on. What about me? What about Jennifer?" She struggled to maintain her composure. It had become a losing battle.

"I know. This is very hard for you." Gallagher knew it was a weak offer of support, but there was nothing else he could say.

A few seconds passed. It was an uneasy period of silence for Gallagher. He looked away, trying to allow her time to gather herself. Then, Jeanne's face became rigid and her eyes narrowed. With a biting voice she asked, "And what about Bill? Do you think he's an innocent bystander, or should I begin blaming him for what happened to Jennifer?"

"Well, you were right about your suspicions of another woman. She was at the address your sister found on that slip of paper in the trash can. I didn't get a good look at her, but when he's in Washington, my guess is he spends a lot of time with her."

"I'm not the least bit surprised. He always had an eye for younger women. His job and all the traveling gave him plenty of opportunities to fool around." Her tone had shifted from sadness to anger. "That bastard!" she exclaimed. "Maybe if he had been a little more devoted to Jennifer, none of this would have happened!"

Gallagher allowed her to vent, but then tossed her another pearl of information. "I followed him for a while on Sunday. Seems like he's become quite a religious guy. Maybe this tragedy may have caused him to look inward and reexamine his life and priorities."

"Bill? Religious? " she scoffed. "Jennifer had to drag him to church. And on those rare occasions when she got him there, it was only because of the kids."

"You should see him now. He was very much involved in the Mass at a church in Virginia. Seems like he is a member there," Gallagher explained.

"Mass? You mean a Catholic church? Bill and Jennifer belonged to the Methodist Church in Needham. You must be mistaken. Bill Clark wouldn't be caught dead in a Catholic church!"

Gallagher sat up. His back stiffened, almost with a shiver. He tried to sift through the meaning of everything Jeanne Campbell had said. Her last words—"wouldn't be caught dead in a Catholic church"— reverberated through his head.

Just when he thought the search had ended, Gallagher had found another reason to keep digging.

Chapter Twenty-Two

The scene in that church was driving him crazy.

He piddled around all week with meaningless stuff, trying to finish organizing the files in his office and make a few contacts for his new venture with security systems. But who was he kidding? Every thought of this new business unleashed an acute attack of narcolepsy. Gallagher was facing a future of outright boredom. He tried to concentrate, but his mind kept drifting back to Bill Clark, the suddenly Catholic Bill Clark. Something about that picture wasn't right. He must have missed a critical clue. He had to see it again. What did he overlook the first time?

The phone rang. It was Jeanne Campbell. She kept him updated on Bill's schedule. He picked up the phone, eager for some news.

"Gallagher?" she asked.

"Yes, Jeanne ... what have you got for me?"

"I spoke to Bill." She hesitated. Her voice sounded disturbed. "And?"

"You know, I like to check with him every week to see if there's anything I can do for the kids."

"How are they doing?"

"Alright, I guess. But, it's been tough for them ... for all of us. I still can't believe Jennifer's gone."

He had no response. None of the typical trite phrases would work. He encouraged her to get to the important stuff. "How's Bill been acting? Anything new with him?"

"That's my problem. He has too much of a 'life goes on' approach to suit me. Ever since you told me the government was watching him, it's made me look at him differently. I don't trust him one bit. He's such a cold bastard. I wouldn't put anything past him."

"Has he said anything specific to make you suspicious?"

"No, other than the fact that he seems to prefer spending more time in Washington. Especially now that he's got something going on down there. You know what I mean."

"The other woman?"

"Yes. I'd feel better if he just came out and told me. But he's so damn secretive about everything."

"Does he think you know?"

"I doubt it. I try to play along ... help him out with the house ... do some errands. I figure that's the best way to get him to open up and talk and maybe find out if he was involved with Jennifer's murder."

"Stay close to your enemies."

"Exactly."

"But you called ...," he said, trying to get her back on track.

"Yes, to let you know that Bill told me he plans to stay in Washington next weekend. I thought maybe you could..."

"Fly down to Washington and check up on him?"

"You read my mind," she said.

"Don't worry. I'll fly to Washington on Saturday and then drive up to Sterling on Sunday morning. That scene in the church still has me puzzled. I'd like to follow him again and see if he goes back. Maybe there was something I missed the first time around."

"Listen, Gallagher, I know I hired you to find Marcie Williams. But there's more to my sister's murder than the government is revealing. I'm not buying those theories about a terrorist putting that bomb in Bill's car. I'm willing to pay for more of your time. I feel like my sister is talking to me ... telling me to keep looking for the answer. I've got to know the truth about her murder."

Gallagher paused for a few seconds and then responded. "So do I, Jeanne, so do I."

He hung up the phone and stared blankly at the ceiling. Obtaining justice for Jennifer Clark—a woman he had never met—had somehow become an all-consuming focus in his life. Her husband, Bill, was hiding something. Gallagher was convinced that the explanation of Jennifer Clark's murder would be found somewhere in that church. He couldn't wait to get back to Washington.

For the second time, the congregation of worshippers at Our Lady of the Snows Catholic Church would be graced with a very interested observer.

Chapter Twenty-Three

Lou Wilson and Ben Harris had driven through the night from Chicago, which had meant more than twenty hours on the road, stopping only for gas and a quick bite to eat. Flying would have been a lot easier and faster. But they never could have cleared airport security with their cache of weapons. More importantly, when their job was finished, a car was the quickest way to leave the scene. They had even obtained a phony set of Massachusetts license plates and a counterfeit registration sticker. Why draw attention to a car from Illinois?

They checked into a cheap motel in Newton, on Route 30. For two guys unfamiliar with Boston, it was a great location. Easy access to the major roads leading into and out of the city. Especially, out of the state.

Their plans had been carefully thought out. The only thing to decide was the precise time and the place. In just a matter of days, it would all be over. They would slip into the night, far away from detection, and be home before the cold bodies were discovered.

Lou Wilson knew he was the brains of this twosome, which is why he called all the shots. He placed his bag on the bed near the window. "I'll take this rack, Ben. I like to sleep where there's a view."

His physically intimidating partner shrugged his shoulders. "I don't give a shit where I sleep. I just wish I had my own room so I could entertain a few local broads tonight."

"Hey," Lou shot back, "None of that stuff while we're here. Remember, we don't make any unnecessary acquaintances. We keep a low profile. Nobody knows us. That's how I want it to stay. You'll have plenty of dough for women when we're done with this job."

The man with the shaved head, wiry mustache, and goatee didn't seem pleased but had no response. He tossed his duffle bag onto the floor and threw himself on the unoccupied bed. "I need a couple hours of shut-eye before we get on with this. Get me up at noon."

Lou ignored him as he quietly unpacked his bag and hung some shirts in the closet. He removed a 9mm Glock automatic pistol from between the layers of socks and underwear. He inspected it for a few seconds and then placed it carefully under the pillow on his bed.

Lou was an organized person—a man of great discipline and focus. He left nothing to chance. He had assembled the plan, the weapons, and a fearsome, ruthless accomplice to assist him. *This guy Gallagher is overmatched. He has no idea what's waiting for him.*

Chapter Twenty-Four

Sunday morning couldn't come soon enough. Gallagher positioned himself once again in the parking area of the Village on Potomac Shores about fifty yards away from the Devonshire Building. He was operating on the premise that people are creatures of habit. He had also verified that there were no changes in the Mass schedule at Our Lady of the Snows: Sundays, 10:30 AM and Noon. So, here he was at eleven-thirty in the morning with his eyes fixed on Unit 4-B, waiting for the door to open.

He wasn't disappointed. About twenty minutes before noon, Bill Clark walked out to his car and drove to the main road. Gallagher followed, but it was almost academic. He knew Clark's destination.

A few minutes before noon, Clark sat alone in a pew on the left side of the center aisle of the church. Gallagher cautiously sat in the rear—out of Clark's sight but in a position where he could observe his every move. Once again, Clark participated in all phases of the Mass, staring straight ahead, never acknowledging any of the other parishioners. During the Offertory he placed an envelope in the collection basket.

Gallagher was so intent on watching the actions of Clark that the presence of the usher holding the basket practically under Gallagher's chin jolted him back to reality. Gallagher reached into his pants pocket and dropped a fresh twenty dollar bill into the basket. He briefly mused that this was another one of those non-reimbursable expenditures.

But then it struck him. *An envelope! Clark had also placed an envelope into the collection basket the last time I was here.*

At the Homily, the parishioners formed two lines down the center aisle as they waited to receive communion. Clark stood on the left, in the line leading up to the celebrant priest. Gallagher checked the Sunday church bulletin—it was the same priest who read Mass on Gallagher's previous visit to Our Lady of the Snows: Monsignor Joseph McGlynn.

Then, an interesting thing happened. Monsignor McGlynn returned to the altar to refill his chalice. His assistant, dispensing communion hosts to those on the right, had an ample supply. Many of the parishioners in the left line moved over to the right to avoid waiting. Clark, however, remained on the left and waited for the Monsignor to return with more hosts. After receiving communion, Clark slowly walked to his seat and bowed his head for a minute.

At the end of the Mass, Clark left the church without speaking to anyone. Gallagher delayed for a while and then waited outside, hoping to catch a few words with the usher who had taken up the collection on Clark's side of the aisle.

The usher, a short man who must have been in his late seventies, walked out to the front steps a few minutes after all of the parishioners had gone. He had a round face, gray hair, and silver-framed glasses.

Gallagher had already taken a notepad and pen out of his jacket pocket and, now, with his best impersonation as a newspaper reporter, approached the man. "Good afternoon. I'm doing a feature article in the Sunday *Post* about some of the most well-known, but unrecognized volunteers in America. Church ushers are fairly high up on our list."

"Really? Church ushers?" replied the man, taken aback by the unexpected compliment.

"Yes. You guys give a lot of time to support your church. You're more important than many people think."

Clearly flattered, the man took a modest approach with his answer. "Well, it's really pretty easy. It just takes some time and you have to keep to your scheduled Mass. If you can't make it for some reason or another, you have to find a replacement. Sometimes it means attending two Masses on a Sunday if you're fillin' in for somebody, but none of us mind."

"Just as I thought. You're a dedicated group."

"Well, we do our best to help out."

"What's the most excitement you've ever had? Any emergencies?" Gallagher held his pen up to the notepad as if poised to jot down the facts.

"Had to call 911 a few times over the years. A couple of people fainted on hot days, and a man had a heart attack one time. Thank God, he was alright after he got to the hospital. All of us are trained in CPR just in case."

"Then there's the weekly collection. That's a responsibility in itself," Gallagher said, opening the door to the main purpose of this discussion.

The older man turned down his lower lip and shrugged his shoulders. "Oh yeah, but we just follow the rules laid down by the diocese."

"Rules? I never realized there were rules. Tell me about them."

"Each collection of the Offertory is placed in a secured bag. The bags are labeled according to which Mass they came from. No usher can handle the bags alone. You have to work in teams."

"Teams?"

"Yes. You never know what could happen if one person had his hands on the money. In fact, you read about that sometimes in the newspapers."

"What happens to the bags?" Gallagher continued to probe.

"The usher team takes them to the rectory and puts them into the drop safe."

"Are the contents of the bags counted on Sundays?"

The man shook his head side to side a few times. "No, the ladies Sodality group sends three members over on Mondays. They open the bags, count the money, and make up the deposit."

"So I guess the ladies from the Sodality have the combination for the safe?"

"Oh, no ...," the man went on. "Only the Monsignor has the combination. He's the only one that can open the safe."

"As an usher, do you get to know all of the parishioners?"

"Pretty much. It's a relatively small parish we've got here. But there are some people at every Mass that you don't recognize. Could be visitors, tourists, or people traveling. Doesn't matter, though. If they're Catholics, they're all welcome."

"The people with envelopes, are they all regular members?" Gallagher asked, as he dutifully jotted down all of the details like any good reporter preparing for his story.

"Yes, and we post their donations according to the number on their envelope. If they ever need it for tax purposes, we have a record of their contributions."

"Do you come across any of the faithful who use envelopes but are not regular members?"

"Matter of fact, there was a guy here today at the noon Mass. Only see him once in a while. Always sits on the left side of the aisle. But always drops his envelope in the basket."

"Ever talk to him?" Gallagher asked. He sensed that he was honing in on the critical facts but was careful to downplay his enthusiasm.

"No, not really. Sort of keeps to himself. Sometimes leaves right after communion, and he doesn't always stay for the end of the Mass or any of the announcements. Never saw him at any church function other than Sunday Mass. But, he's a nice contributor to the church."

"How do you know that?"

"He drops at least one envelope into the basket every time he comes to Mass. Sometimes, two. Guess he likes to make up for weeks when he's out of town and can't be there. We could use more members like him. The church really needs the money. This is a tough time for Our Lady," the man stated.

"How come? Does the church have financial problems?"

"They're threatening to close us. Part of a consolidation effort by the bishop. The Monsignor's doing everything he can to keep us afloat, but we need more donations. The cost to run a church is higher than most people think."

Gallagher picked up on a new line of questioning. "Has the Monsignor been here a long time?"

"About ten years. What a great man. Very dedicated to helping poor people in all parts of the world. Goes on a missionary trip a few times a year," the man marveled.

"That's quite admirable. Where does he go?"

"He's been to a lot of places ... South America, Africa, India ... you name it. But for the past year he's been going to a place where I wouldn't dare travel. Gotta give him credit. There's plenty of danger in some of those trips. And, mind you, I served in the Korean War, so there's not much that scares me."

"Where's this dangerous place he's traveling to?"

"Monsignor McGlynn is a missionary for the UN World Food program. They take food and medical supplies to North Korea."

Gallagher tried to act cool, but he almost dropped his pen when he heard the last two words. *North Korea,* he mused to himself. *Of all places, North Korea!!*

Gallagher thanked the man for the interview and politely took his name and address. "Be sure to look in the *Post* sometime in the next few weeks for the story. I might make you famous," he joked as he walked toward his car. Gallagher hated to take advantage of the old guy, especially a veteran, which was a group of men for whom he had the greatest respect.

But this was a war in itself. The normal rules of engagement had to be ignored. Someone was responsible for the death of Jennifer Clark.

Gallagher wouldn't give this up until he could prove who killed her.

Chapter Twenty-Five

It was a masterful plan.

Gallagher had to give credit to Bill Clark for coming up with it. Knowing that his actions would be under scrutiny by investigators from the NSA and the Department of Defense, Clark had devised a way to transfer highly classified information to a courier who would never be suspected of treason—a Catholic priest who was a missionary to the poor. Someone who could travel to South Korea and then cross the border into North Korea under the protection of the United Nations!

Clark's clever system never allowed anyone to catch him red-handed in a transaction with a foreign agent or in the process of delivering the ciphers of top-secret government messages. He simply placed the code-breaking information in a donation envelope for Our Lady of the Snows and then dropped the envelope in the collection basket on Sunday.

His presence in the communion line was a signal to Monsignor McGlynn that a drop had occurred. Then sometime later, before the women arrived to open the collection bags, the Monsignor retrieved Clark's marked envelopes from the safe.

Why would a priest become involved with such highly treasonous acts?

Gallagher assumed that the promise of substantial anonymous donations to the church was a critical factor in the rationalization process. Furthermore, the decidedly liberal, peace-loving philosophy of the Church encouraged a balance of world power. Perhaps the transfer of this information would level the international playing field, reduce the threat of nuclear war, and eventually bring about peace between North Korea and its antagonistic neighbors. Whatever lay beneath his motivation, Gallagher was sure that Monsignor McGlynn served as the clandestine conduit of information to North Korea.

In the meantime, Bill Clark had developed his own secret money stream—undoubtedly getting rich from payoffs for the code-breaking formulas he supplied.

But a much larger issue loomed for Gallagher.

Was Bill Clark getting away with murder?

Chapter Twenty-Six

Gallagher was true to his word. He knew the information he uncovered was out of his domain and should be turned over to the CIA, as he had promised Rebecca Johnson. It was late on Sunday afternoon when he flipped his phone open and pressed her cell number.

"Becky? It's Gallagher."

The voice on the other end of the call seemed surprised, almost hesitant to respond. "Gallagher ...I wasn't sure if I'd ever be hearing from you again."

"Listen, I've found out a few things that you should know."

"Okay, you've got my attention. Let's hear it."

"I think I know how Bill Clark is getting information out of the country."

"Really?" she said. She sounded skeptical.

"He stays in a townhouse with his mistress in Sterling, Virginia. I actually tracked her down through an address Jennifer discovered about six months before she was killed."

"How did you get the address?"

"Jennifer showed it to Jeanne. For some reason, Jeanne just held on to it. Thought it might be important some day if Bill decided to divorce Jennifer."

"So, he's got a girlfriend. Am I supposed to get real excited? You said it yourself. A lot of these guys fool around."

"Wait, there's much more. Bill's been attending Mass at a Catholic church not far from there. I believe Clark is feeding government secrets to a priest from the church."

"A priest?"

"Not just any priest, he just happens to be a regular traveler to North Korea … volunteers as a missionary from the UN."

"Seems pretty far-fetched. Are you sure about all of this?"

"It all fits together. Maybe this is why your investigators could never catch him in the act. Did anyone ever wonder why a part-time Methodist from Massachusetts would suddenly start going to a Catholic church in Virginia? This can't be a coincidence."

"Have you told this theory to anyone else?" she asked.

"No. I just wanted to talk to you first."

"You did the right thing. What else can you tell me?"

"Well, the church is Our Lady of the Snows. The priest is Monsignor Joseph McGlynn. Got that?"

"Yes, I'm writing it down." She paused briefly and then picked up the conversation with a stern tone in her voice. "Look, Gallagher. What you're saying could be critical to national security. If Clark is guilty, and this is his angle, we don't want him to know that we're on to him."

"I hear you," he said.

"We need to stop him, but we also need to verify his contacts, both in and out of the country. We want to permanently close the channel of leaks. So …listen carefully … don't share your suspicions with anyone. It's essential that you keep this information to yourself." Her admonishment was firm, but reasonable in its intent.

"Don't worry. I understand where you're coming from. As I said before, I'll leave the spy versus spy stuff for you. Just keep in mind that Jeanne Campbell ultimately wants to know what happened to her sister. I want your word that, in return, you'll share any information about the car bombing with us."

"It's a deal. Thanks Gallagher. We'll get right on this."

"Good."

"By the way, are you still in Washington?" she asked.

"Yes. But, I'm leaving for Boston later tonight."

"Okay." She paused for a second. "Listen ... Gallagher. It's good that you contacted me. I do appreciate this information. Be sure to call me if you find out anything else."

"No problem. I will."

"Have a safe trip," she said as she clicked off the phone.

Chapter Twenty-Seven

Rebecca's demeanor changed suddenly after she hung up. She stood up and began pacing around the room. The calm, carefully measured temperament she had displayed during her phone conversation with Gallagher now erupted into an outburst of rage. She pounded her fist aimlessly in the air and then threw her cellular phone wildly into the cushions on the couch. "Damn him!" she screamed, but there was no one to witness her anger.

She gradually regained her composure, retrieved her cell, and pressed a single digit on her speed dial list. She lit a cigarette, inhaled deeply, and continued her nervous, emotional pace around the room.

After two rings a man's voice answered the call. "Yes," he said.

Rebecca spoke slowly and clearly to ensure there would be no misunderstanding of her words.

"I need to see you. We've got a problem."

Chapter Twenty-Eight

The weekends were the toughest for Kate, and this was a Sunday night. On Monday through Friday, she had work to occupy her time and her mind. The head-hunting agency she operated with her partner was getting busier with each quarter of the fiscal year. The daily schedule of interviews and appointments often stretched into the early evening. When she got back to her parents' home at the Cape, she was usually exhausted and went to sleep early.

The self-imposed exile from her husband was even harder than she had thought it would be. Sure, he called frequently to keep her from worrying. But she missed him terribly and longed for the day when this latest job would be over. Would they be able to get back together again?

His attraction to these cases was maddening. Would he ever get it out of his system? The seductive danger, the intrigue, the constant pecking away at minute details to uncover a larger, hidden truth. Those were the magnets he found so intoxicating, like an addictive drug. Yes, Gallagher, her husband, was an investigating junkie.

His absence, however, made her realize that she loved him more than ever. She missed the closeness of his body and the intimate moments they shared. Their married life had just begun. All of the momentum of loving togetherness had come to a grinding halt because of this case—another that he couldn't resist. She loved and cursed him simultaneously.

Forever etched in her mind was the frightening, nearly-deadly experience in Gallagher's condominium at Bay View Towers last year. Two men had forced their way through the front door, tied her to a chair, and held her at gunpoint. She had watched in horror as they placed silencers on their guns and waited for Gallagher to come home—to kill him because he had uncovered the truth about the West Castle murder case.

She and her husband were fortunate to escape. She vowed to never allow them to go through an experience like that again. He had promised to give up his business as a private investigator. Now this. Was it truly the last case?

During his phone calls, he discussed very little about the circumstances of the current investigation. He always reminded her that he was not at risk and that he relied on government specialists to handle matters out of his realm. He promised that soon it would be over, she would feel safe, and they could resume their life together.

Kate Gallagher, alone in her bed and unable to sleep, wondered if that day would ever come.

Chapter Twenty-Nine

The office of Tom Manzelli, Deputy Director of the CIA, was one of the plushest in CIA headquarters. In addition to the handsome desk of dark cherry wood and the high-backed leather chair that oozed luxurious comfort, the corner office had a wonderful view of the outdoor courtyard and gardens. This was among the many privileges he enjoyed as a result of rising through the ranks to a top position in one of the world's most secretive governmental agencies.

Rebecca Johnson appreciated many of Tom Manzelli's attributes. She admired his distinguished appearance: slightly gray at the temples and always dressed with a neatly pressed shirt, tailored slacks, and a brightly colored tie. His almost business-like image made one think that he had spent his entire career sitting behind a desk, having never gotten his hands dirty. But Rebecca knew that this look belied the fact that he was a hardened veteran of Cold-War encounters with Russian agents. He had faced adversity and overcome it. He had told her stories about how he had been challenged, only to emerge as the winner. She loved the way he could seize opportunity and not let it escape.

Sitting across from him at seven-thirty in the evening, Rebecca could not hide the worried look on her face. "He knows about our drop and where the information's going," she started.

"Shit!" said Manzelli disgustedly. "How did he find out?"

"He's relentless. You saw how he followed me for three days. He probably did the same to Clark and somehow figured it out."

"But, he trusts you?"

"Yes, he bought my whole story. In fact, I think he'll call me with any new revelations."

"Has he talked to anyone else? Is he the kind of guy who keeps records on all of this?"

"I don't think so, but I can't be sure."

"This is no time for uncertainty, Becky. We have to know."

"All I can say is there's something about this guy that worries me. He may know more than he's letting on."

"Then we've got to take him out."

"How?"

"In one of the usual ways. Have one of our special agents take him for a long ride. Someone will find him in the woods. You might be a good choice for that assignment."

"Why me?" she asked.

"Because you've got experience in these delicate matters."

"And what about Clark?"

"He's served his usefulness. He's got to go before he panics and cracks. We had a hard enough time keeping him under control after the car bombing."

"That just leaves us with the "good" Monsignor?"

"I'll make sure he's intercepted at the border at Panmunjom. We'll get the word to Kyung Kim. Someone smuggling information out of the North who resists arrest…," he smiled, letting his devious thought crystallize in her mind. "Such people are treated very harshly. I'm sure there'll be a big fuss for a while, but it will die down in time. It's certainly not going to cause a declaration of war."

She crossed her legs, allowing her skirt to ride high up on her thighs. She breathed a deep sigh, almost in despair. But it was a mock gesture. She looked across at his eyes; they were consumed with the provocative view below her waist. "Then you're left to deal with me," she said mischievously.

"You, Becky? Oh no, I would never get rid of you."

Chapter Thirty

Done. As in one hundred percent finished. That was the agreement Gallagher had made with Kate. He would not ask her to return to their home until he had completely taken himself off this case. No loose ends to tie up and no further searches. After his conversation with Rebecca Johnson, he felt that he needed a few more days to see how everything played out. Had he given her enough information to close in on Bill Clark and arrest him for treason? Would his arrest provide answers to the mystery of the car-bombing incident?

Gallagher returned to Boston on a late flight Sunday evening. By the time he got to his car in the parking area of Terminal B and drove out to their home in Needham, it was almost midnight. As he approached the driveway, he pressed the button for the automatic garage door opener. He slowly pulled into the garage and pressed the button again, closing the door behind him.

The high-pitched beeping noise of the alarm system greeted him as he opened the door from the garage. He entered the four-digit security code on the keypad to disarm the system. He waited a few seconds and then entered a seven-digit code that was used to block the interior motion detectors but still sound a loud alert if a door or window was opened. He had no plans to leave again for the evening.

He went to the refrigerator, took out a bottle of sparkling water, and poured himself a drink. There was one message on the answering machine—from Diane with the phone number of a client who called for information about his business proposal.

Tired from all of the travel in the past few days, he trudged into the bedroom and collapsed on the bed. Too late for email or a response to the message on the answering machine. He would deal with all of that tomorrow when he got to his office. Besides, he had an important visit planned for tomorrow; a visit that he hoped would answer more of his questions about Jennifer Clark's murder.

He turned on the television for the late news but soon clicked on the sleep button of the remote control. Within a few minutes he was sound asleep.

A solitary figure had been peering into Gallagher's bedroom window. He slowly retreated from the house and moved quietly down the street.

Chapter Thirty-One

The Massachusetts Correctional Institution at Shirley is a medium-security prison located approximately forty miles northwest of Boston. Gallagher drove west on Route 2 and exited just past Fort Devens, a former Army base that had since been converted to a multiuse complex that included Red Tail, a championship golf course. He turned right off the exit ramp and entered the parking area of the correctional facility.

This was his first visit to this prison. He had not seen the inmate he was calling upon for more than three years. But they had a connection from the past. Gallagher was counting on that connection to provide answers to a question that would not go away.

As required, he had made the appointment several days ago, fulfilling the minimum notice of twenty-four hours in advance. No last minute visitors were allowed. He dressed in a pair of navy blue slacks and a light blue shirt with a button-down collar—abiding by the visitors' strict dress code that was posted on the prison's web site as well as at the entrance: no denim or dungaree pants; no sweatshirts or workout clothes; no coats, jackets, or vests. And no neck ties, unless you were an attorney.

A guard escorted Gallagher to a row of chairs separated by a Plexiglas window from a similar row on the other side. He took a seat and waited. A few minutes later, another prison guard accompanied a man in his mid-thirties into the room and pointed to the seat opposite

Gallagher. The guard retreated through the door at the rear and left the two men to talk alone.

Dougie Mannion—only five feet six and weighing less than one hundred and fifty pounds—was serving an eight-year sentence for a variety of offenses, including armed robbery, arson, and possession of cocaine. Gallagher had last seen Mannion when the private detective sat in a courtroom with Dougie's mother and sister as a judge announced his sentence. The inmate's shaggy blonde hair was now trimmed very close to the scalp. From the look of other inmates in the room, Gallagher assumed that Dougie had received the standard prison haircut. Despite his many encounters with the law and the hard times he must have endured in prison, Dougie had retained the boyish appearance Gallagher remembered. The dimples on his cheeks gave a decidedly Irish look to his beaming smile.

"Hey, Gallagher. I couldn't believe it when I saw your name on the visitors' list. What's the story? Are you bringing me a Christmas present? Or did you find some new evidence that gets me outta here?"

"Sorry Dougie. It's just a friendly visit. Need your help with something."

"You need my help?" Dougie asked with a wide-eyed, animated smile as he pointed his finger into his chest. "How am I going to help you from this place? I've still got five years to go and I'm strugglin' to stay alive."

"I need to tap into your area of expertise. I want to ask you a few questions about rigging a car bomb."

"Man, the private eye business is really branching out!" Dougie roared. "Whattya' wanna do, end up in here as my bunk mate?"

"No, I'll pass on that, Dougie. I'm working on a case that involves a woman who was killed by a bomb planted in her husband's car."

"Was he killed, too?" The subject matter had turned serious. Dougie dropped the wisecracks.

"No, she was alone."

"So you think the guy might have set her up?"

"That's what I'm trying to determine. How hard is it to rig a car that way?"

Dougie's face became solemn. He was a master of this trade and began speaking like a clinical instructor. "That all depends on who's involved. First, you've gotta have the right materials. You don't just walk into Home Depot, look in the dynamite section, and ask one of the clerks to point you toward the mercury fulminate and blasting caps. You've gotta know where to get this stuff."

"Where could someone living in this area buy the materials?" asked Gallagher.

"You won't find it in the yellow pages. Guys like me who were in that business know these things. Word gets around. I'd rather not give out any names."

"Then, assuming you have the right materials, how long does it take to hook them up to the car?"

"Again, it all depends. For a guy like you, with some basic knowledge about cars ... maybe half an hour. But it's a little complicated, and you might blow your fingers off while you're messin' around with the wiring. For someone like me, maybe five minutes," Dougie said proudly. He paused for emphasis and then added, "Tops."

Gallagher was well aware of Dougie's prowess in this area. Arson had been one of his specialties. The prosecutor at his trial cited a number of automobiles and buildings that were torched as part of an insurance scam. Dougie and the owners had split the profits—until an arson investigator figured it all out and nailed the owner of one of the buildings. The owner confessed, cut a deal for himself, and fingered Dougie. Case closed. Eight years in the slammer for Dougie.

But Gallagher couldn't hide his disappointment with the extent of the information being provided today. It showed on his face. He obviously needed much more from his imprisoned friend.

Dougie recognized the problem and slid closer to the small circular grid in the window. Lowering his voice, he started, "Look, Gallagher. I owe you big time. You brought my sister back to my mother before she got herself into trouble. And you didn't charge me a dime. I'll never forget that."

"It's alright, Dougie. Glad I could help you."

Mannion stared at Gallagher for a few seconds without speaking, obviously considering what he was about to say. He blinked several times, appearing to be torn by indecision. He bit his lip nervously, moved even closer to the grid, and then whispered, "There's a guy in Salem, New Hampshire…Chuck Cumming. Runs a fireworks store called Granite Fireworks. He's a mad scientist type and knows all about this shit."

Gallagher took the cue and slid closer to the window. This was the break he had been seeking. "Will he talk to me?" he asked softly.

"No, at first he'll be cautious and probably think you're a cop. But tell him you're my friend and that I remember Bernadette. Got that? Bernadette. No cop would know what that means. Say that name to Chuck and he'll give you anything you need."

Dougie leaned away from the vented opening in the glass. He grinned across at his friend, knowing that, on this occasion, he was the one who had come through—big time. Gallagher nodded his head and smiled, acknowledging that he had carefully logged this latest information into his memory bank.

Bernadette … Bernadette … I wonder what that name means? thought Gallagher.

In a few more minutes their brief encounter was over. A buzzer sounded, signaling the end of the allotted visiting time. Dougie stood up, waiting for the guard to escort him out of the room.

"Take care of yourself, Dougie," said Gallagher, with a tone of sadness in his voice. Five more years in this place. So much could happen to ruin a young man in that time. He wondered if Dougie would be able to survive, serve out his sentence, eventually get a job, and avoid the risks of a life of crime.

"Don't worry about me, Gallagher. I'll be all right. You're the one who has to watch his ass," Dougie said.

Chapter Thirty-Two

When Diane took her key out of the lock and entered the office, she knew immediately that something was wrong. The cardboard boxes that had been carefully filled with files and neatly stacked in the outer office were spilled onto the floor. Papers were strewn all over the top of her desk, and the drawers were pulled open.

What happened here? Who did this? she said to herself.

Knowing that someone had broken into the office and violated her personal space was chilling in itself. But the fact that this person had gained access to intimate details of her boss's clients troubled her even more.

The door to Gallagher's private office was ajar, and she could visualize a similar scene of disruption. Her worried, rambling thoughts continued. *Who could have been here? Why would someone have interest in rummaging through the files? What had this person been looking for?*

She cautiously walked to the doorway to get a better view of Gallagher's private office. Something was definitely not right here. She began to grow fearful but was not prepared for the horrific sight that awaited her. The light-colored Berber carpet had a smattering of brownish-red spots. She leaned down to examine the spots more closely. They were moist—blood stains.

Her heartbeat quickened. She wanted to run out of the office and scream for help, but a sense of duty and loyalty forced her to deal with this intrusion on her own. The office was frighteningly silent. *Is it always so quiet here or am I just imagining this?*

In an instant her eyes followed the trail of stains to the far side of Gallagher's desk. First, she saw the shoes—then the legs—then the entire torso. More blood. A lot more blood.

Oh, my God! Something terrible has happened! A man's body was lying on the floor. She was afraid to look at his face.

Diane put her hand to her mouth and slowly backed away until she reached the doorway to the private office. Then she turned and moved quickly toward the telephone on her desk. She picked up the phone and called the police.

Chapter Thirty-Three

Diane's frantic call came as he drove east on the Mass Pike toward Boston. He had left the prison in Shirley just a half hour earlier. Certainly, the news that a dead body had been found in his office provided an incentive for Gallagher to drive a little faster than his usual speed.

What the hell is going on here? His mind was racing with wild possibilities. *A dead man in my office? What was he looking for? Who killed him? Could this be related to Bill Clark and the mysterious transfer of secret government information to North Korea? Should I call Rebecca Johnson to inform her?*

When he arrived at his office a combination of bedlam and commotion greeted him. A uniformed officer stopped him at the door. "This is a crime scene. No one is allowed in here," he barked.

"This is my office!" Gallagher snapped back, taking out his wallet and showing his license to the officer to verify his identity.

The officer held one hand against Gallagher's chest to keep him from entering and used his other to point to a man in a blue suit. "Stay right here. You have to speak to Detective Phillips. He's from Homicide. He's in charge."

The man in the blue suit overheard the conversation and motioned towards Gallagher. "Let him in. We have some questions for Mr. Gallagher," he said as he waved his arm.

The office was filled with police personnel. A man in plain clothes stood in the private office and took photographs from various angles. His camera pointed downward at the floor. Gallagher assumed correctly that the body was still there.   Diane sat calmly at her desk answering questions from another detective. Gallagher loved her resiliency under such trying circumstances. He walked over, leaned down, and gave her an emotional hug. "Are you all right?" he asked.

"Don't worry. I'm fine," she replied. "Just a little frazzled."

Detective Phillips, a gray-haired man, turned away from the other police officers who were standing with him and directed his attention toward Gallagher. "Bruce Phillips, Homicide," he said as he extended his hand

Gallagher shook his hand and replied, "Gallagher." Then, with a puzzled look, he asked, "What happened here?"

"Maybe you should be telling us," said Phillips flatly.

"All I know is what Diane told me when she called. Someone evidently broke in and went through my files. Whoever it was left a dead man on the floor."

Phillips looked at him suspiciously and replied coldly, "Follow me." He motioned with his head toward the back office and led the way as Gallagher walked closely behind him.

They walked to the side of the desk. A black tarpaulin cover had been placed over the motionless figure that was lying on the carpet. Phillips leaned down and pulled the cover down past the shoulders of the corpse, exposing the left side of the dead man's face and neck.

The man was clean shaven with close-cropped, brown hair, neatly parted and combed to the side. His eyes were closed but his mouth appeared fixed in a macabre, half-open position. Rigor mortis had already set in. A wide ring of blood had stained the carpet and extended away from underneath the body. Gallagher assumed that the man had been shot in the chest while standing near his desk and then staggered, fell to the floor, and landed on his stomach.

Gallagher's intense assessment of the gruesome sight was interrupted by Phillip's impatient demand. "Well ... do you know this guy?"

"Never saw him before. Who is he?"

"We don't have an ID. His wallet was taken. No car keys, no nothing. But he doesn't look like your run-of-the-mill night burglar. He was here for a reason and someone evidently walked in on him."

"Or maybe he had a partner and something happened," offered Gallagher, trying to consider all of the possible scenarios.

Phillips put his lips together and then forcibly exhaled through his mouth, scoffing at Gallagher's suggestion, and quickly moved ahead with another question. "Where were you last night?"

"Home in bed. Got back late from a trip out of town."

"Were you alone?"

"Yes."

"No alibi … that figures." Gallagher chose to ignore the implication and stood impassively, waiting for Phillip's next salvo. A clear line had been drawn in the sand—these two just didn't like each other.

Phillips continued, "I assume, as a private investigator, you have a registered gun."

"Right."

"Where is it?"

"It's locked in the wall safe behind that picture." Gallagher pointed to the picture of Jason Varitek putting a strangle hold on Alex Rodriquez during a Red Sox-Yankees confrontation in the 2004 playoffs.

"I see you're a Sox fan," said Phillips. It seemed like every statement had some probing purpose.

"Isn't everybody?" deadpanned Gallagher.

Phillips ignored his reply. "If you don't mind, we'll take the gun just to make sure it didn't fire the bullet into this guy." Phillips's casual manner indicated his confidence that the gun was not involved. Gallagher walked over to the wall safe, opened it, removed the .38 Smith & Wesson revolver and turned it over to the detective.

Gallagher knew this routine. What else could he expect? When an unidentified dead body shows up in your office, you're bound to come under some degree of suspicion. Why not cooperate and let it all play out?

Phillips then continued with his questions. "Why would this guy break in here? What kind of cases are you involved with these days? Looking into the wrong peepholes? Collecting dirt on some rich guy?"

Phillips's disdain for private investigators was now clearly in the open. Gallagher stayed cool, not wanting to fuel the fire but also unwilling to share too much with this buffoon.

"Nothing that would be of real interest to anyone. In fact, I'm in the process of closing the office."

"What's in all the boxes?"

"Just files and photos from my old cases. We're getting them ready to go into storage. Looks like I've got a lot of repacking to do."

"Who would be so interested in what you've got in these files?"

"Ask the dead man. He's the only one who knows the answer to that question."

Phillips dour expression was a sign that he didn't appreciate the wisecrack. Gesturing toward the body on the floor, however, he replied with a quip of his own, "He's obviously unable to talk right now. Someone made sure of that."

Then, he moved closer to Gallagher, almost nose to nose with his newfound antagonist. Gallagher was all too familiar with police intimidation tactics like this one and firmly stood his ground. Phillips challenged him, "You must know something about this. You wouldn't be holding back anything, would you Mr. Private Eye?"

"Not at all. I have no idea who this guy is or why he was here."

Phillips retreated a few feet, but it looked like he was still sizing up his competition. Probably he knew Gallagher was being evasive but had no way to force him to provide more information. "We'll run his prints, picture, and DNA. It may take a few days, but we'll find out who he is. And then we may have some more questions for you. Stick around, Gallagher. We don't want to launch an APB to pick you up."

The photographs, measurements, and detailed examination of the office continued for almost an hour. A team of two forensic specialists meticulously collected samples of debris from the carpet, desk, and chairs. All surfaces were dusted for fingerprints. Eventually, three deputies from the coroner's office arrived and removed the body. It was an eerie scene as they placed the tightly wrapped corpse on a gurney and wheeled it out to a van marked "Suffolk County: Office of the Medical Examiner."

Gallagher stood quietly off to the side viewing all of the proceedings and trying to come up with an explanation for this latest development.

He made a superficial review of the opened files. Nothing appeared to be missing. None of the cases contained even a hint of incriminating information that would cause someone to break into the office at night and risk being arrested for burglary.

What was this guy looking for? Who shot him? Why, of all places, in my office?

Gallagher waited for Phillips and his investigative crew to leave. He had to make an important phone call. But he needed privacy, and he didn't want to answer any more of Phillips's questions.

In particular, he didn't want to tell Phillips he was calling an agent who worked for the CIA. Gallagher would rather avoid opening that can of worms at this time. Phillips might keep him up all night with more of his interrogation. No, thanks.

Gallagher had plenty of questions of his own. But there was one that had clearly topped his list.

What does Rebecca Johnson know about all of this?

Chapter Thirty-Four

Three days of repeated phone messages and no responses. Gallagher could only reach her voice mail. Either Rebecca Johnson was screening her calls, refusing to speak to him, or she had gone off on another assignment for the CIA where she was completely incommunicado.

Gallagher's frustration with his inability to determine the cause of the break-in and the identity of the dead man was beginning to show. His coffee intake actually increased beyond the usual level of caffeine overload. He felt edgy and vulnerable. He needed answers.

He called Jeanne Campbell to inform her of the incident at his office and get the latest reading on Bill Clark's itinerary. Her response did little to improve his mental state. "Sorry, I haven't heard from Bill in a few days. I've tried his cell phone, but I'm getting no answer. His office line sends me right to voice mail, and he hasn't returned my calls. I spoke to Marissa at school. She hasn't had a call from him in a while. He's either buried in his work or, for some reason, has decided to avoid the world." Gallagher didn't want to say it, but wondered if the operative word in her sentence was "buried."

Rebecca Johnson and Bill Clark. Both unavailable. Could they be missing? A dead man was found in my office just days after I told Rebecca my theories about Bill Clark and his holy accomplice.

Gallagher's mind kept churning out possibilities, but he wasn't able to make the right connection. He sat at his desk in his Commercial

Street office mulling over these thoughts and idly looking through his mail, mostly the usual assortment of junk mail, credit card offers and utility bills. The pile included one plain envelope addressed to him and marked "Personal." There was no return address. The postmark read "Washington D.C."

He tore open the flap and removed an index card from the inside of the envelope. Taped to the index card was an automobile key—the type of spare key that could be carried in a wallet. Gallagher studied the key and flipped the index card over and over again. There were neither instructions nor an address enclosed.

A blank car key? Why would someone send me a key?

Chapter Thirty-Five

When Gallagher finally got a call, it was not the one he expected. The number on the screen of his cellular was unfamiliar. He flipped the phone open and took it anyway.

"Gallagher here."

"This is Bruce Phillips, Boston Homicide. We've got some information we'd like to share with you. How soon can you get down to police headquarters?"

Gallagher glanced at his watch and then replied. "Probably half an hour."

"That would be great. You know where to find me?"

"Of course, I used to work there. You must have checked my background to know I was a Boston cop."

"Oh yeah, we know all about you, Gallagher. Maybe more than you think. See you in a few minutes," said Phillips as he clicked off the phone.

Boston Police Headquarters is a large, impressive building of granite, glass, and steel that is located in the Roxbury Crossing section of Boston adjacent to Southwest Corridor Park. Gallagher arrived at the main entrance at One Schroeder Plaza within twenty minutes of Phillips's phone call. After clearing through security in the lobby, he took the stairs to the second floor and walked into Phillips's office.

Phillips sat behind his desk, flanked by two other detectives who were there for more than just moral support. The serious expressions on their faces told Gallagher he was in for a major inquisition. Phillips wasted no time getting to his point. "Sit down, Gallagher, and tell us what you know about Mark Fleming."

"Is he the guy you found in my office?"

"Yes."

"Never heard the name before. Don't know anything about him."

Phillips continued with his pronouncements, cautiously eyeing Gallagher and waiting for a reaction. "A meter maid spotted a car parked down the street from your office. It was left there for a couple of days accumulating tickets. We ran a check on the car, and it was registered in Fleming's name. We also ran the fingerprints of the dead man. Bingo! Fleming again."

Gallagher sensed the tone of the meeting and was aware of the penetrating eyes that were focused upon him, hoping for a crack in his comportment. He replied cautiously, "Good work, Detective. But I don't know the guy."

Phillips went on, like an actor relishing the stage, knowing he had a great punch line to deliver. "We did some further checking on Fleming and found that he had some very interesting credentials. Most recently, he was a freelance investigator. Doing sort of the work you do but on special cases or assignments. Mostly corporate stuff. He had a lot of experience in government work before he set out on his own. Must have had some good contacts."

"What did he do for the government?" asked Gallagher, his curiosity now raised by the dead man's background, but he was not prepared for Phillips's next proclamation that nearly startled him out of his chair.

"Mark Fleming used to be employed by the CIA."

Gallagher paused for a few seconds and stared at Phillips. He knew the two other detectives were mentally recording his reaction to the news—watching his mannerisms, how often he blinked, or any other signs that he was becoming unglued. *Forget it, boys. I'm not giving anything away.*

"The CIA?" he said. "They'd be wasting their time in my office. Whatever this guy Fleming was looking for, I doubt that he found it. Have you thought of questioning Diane? Maybe she shot him for making such a mess of her desk."

Gallagher's flip attitude sparked Phillips's ire and he abruptly stood up from his chair and ended the meeting. "We're not done with you, Gallagher. Eventually we'll figure this out. And when we do, I just might be slapping a pair of handcuffs on you. You'd better not be hiding any evidence," he warned.

Reversing the tables, Gallagher came back with a question of his own. "That reminds me, Detective Phillips, what did the ballistics tests show? I assume you determined that my gun was not the murder weapon."

"You can pick up your gun in the Crime Lab," Phillips barked. He motioned to one of the detectives in the room. "Take him downstairs and escort him the hell out of here," he said as he made a sweeping motion toward the door with his arm.

Gallagher's bravado had succeeded in getting Phillips off his back, at least temporarily. It was way too early to bring the local police into this complicated federal matter. Detective Phillips and his brazen style could only hamper Gallagher's investigation. Even worse, the door would be opened to questions about Jennifer Clark's private life, which was an area that, for the present time, Gallagher felt duty bound to protect.

The fact that the dead man was linked to the CIA had added an entirely new level of complexity and danger to a case that had started as a simple search for a woman who had gone missing. He needed a little breathing space to sort out the ramifications of this latest bombshell.

But, where is Rebecca Johnson? She must know something about the dead man. I might have to go back to Washington to find her again. Do I dare tell Kate about this? And what about that strange key? Who sent it to me and why? These questions were ricocheting around his head as he walked to his car.

However, the stark reality of the situation began to set in. Gallagher adjusted the shoulder strap of the holster of his .38 that he'd retrieved from the police and checked to make certain the weapon was in proper working order.

Something made him believe he was going to need it.

Chapter Thirty-Six

Lan Tauber was growing impatient. Three weeks had gone by since his meeting with the two hit men from Chicago and still no results and no indication that they had carried out their assignment. *These guys are supposed to be good. What are they waiting for? Did they take my ten grand and screw?*

As he drove from Summerlin toward the Las Vegas Strip in his Cadillac DeVille, his thoughts could not escape the agitation that boiled within him. His reputation was at stake. He knew what others were thinking. The whispers were growing louder. How could he be effective in his role as the primary intimidator for the Syndicate if he could not eliminate the one person who had bested him?

There had been plenty of others who thought they could escape his displeasure. Or, foolishly, try to challenge his position. But each one had failed, and, in failing, they had found themselves belly up in the ground.

This private eye in Boston was a problem in more ways than one. The Feds had apparently given up on implicating Tauber in the West Castle murder case. But what if Gallagher had been pursuing the investigation by himself? Would he seek his own measure of revenge? A personal vendetta against Tauber? After all, Gallagher had been Johnny Nicoletti's target on two different occasions, and he had made it clear afterward that he believed Tauber was somehow linked to the plot to kill him.

Fortunately, the Feds had no proof of Tauber's involvement and wouldn't buy Gallagher's conspiracy theories.   However, Tauber remembered Prendergast's warning that "these guys keep digging until they find something."   Suppose Gallagher turned up evidence that reopened the case?

To let Gallagher survive was not only a sign of weakness but a risk to Tauber's personal safety.   His anonymous employers may fear that Tauber's involvement might eventually jeopardize their own position. Would they decide to eliminate the one man who, in an effort to save himself, could turn state's evidence and testify against them about dozens of crimes committed on their behalf?

The answer to these vexing questions was really quite simple: Gallagher could not be allowed to cause any further problems.   He was a potential liability that required a permanent solution.

Lan Tauber's paranoid ramblings continued.

What are these guys waiting for?

Chapter Thirty-Seven

Gallagher's phone rang at six-thirty in the morning. Normally, he would have just ignored the call and picked up the message later when he was awake and the cobwebs had cleared away. But when he opened one eye and saw her name on the call screen, his adrenaline kicked in, and he immediately sat up in his bed.

"Rebecca?" he said excitedly. "I've been trying to reach you for days."

"Yes, I know. I'm sorry, but there's a reason I haven't been able to call. I've been doing a lot of soul searching and have come to a decision. There's no going back now. I've been involved in some terrible things. It was all wrong. It's time to get out while I can."

She sounded frightened and confused. She was breathing heavily and her voice kept fading in and out. He wondered if he had heard everything she said. "Where are you?" he asked.

"I'm in Washington, but I'm calling from a place where the signal may not be very good. I have to be careful. Can you hear me?"

"Just barely. You sound scared. Tell me what this is all about."

"I am afraid. Afraid for my life and yours. The corruption at NSA and the CIA runs all the way to the top of both agencies. Bill Clark is a mere puppet in a larger plan to sell highly classified material to our enemies. Millions of dollars have been paid out already. They'll resort to any means to keep this story from getting out. That dead man in your office was no accident. You know too much. They're out to get rid of you one way or another."

"Why was he in my office? What was he looking for?"

"Mark Fleming was a former agent at the CIA. He left on poor terms years ago but kept in touch with a lot of his old friends. Once in a while, they hired him for a special assignment. They sent him to search your office to make sure you didn't have any records of your findings about Clark. Something happened—I don't know what, but Fleming ended up dead."

"How do you fit into this? What have you done wrong?"

"I've been part of it all along. Played up to my boss and even gave him information about your phone call to me But they were on to you from the first day you followed me. They just waited to see what you were after and hoped you'd go away. They were suspicious of me after we talked. I had to pretend I was still with them. I wish you had taken my advice and stayed out of this. You put your life on the line."

"So, why the phone call today?"

"I need your help. You're the one person I can trust. There's only one way for both of us to come out of this mess alive."

"What are you proposing?" he asked skeptically.

"I've been wearing a wire to our meetings. I've got recordings of conversations with enough incriminating statements to put all of them behind bars. I'm hoping for a break from the government prosecutors if I turn everything over and testify against them."

"Where do I fit in? What do you want me to do?" he asked.

"I need you to deliver the tapes to the FBI. I'm being watched all the time, and I don't know if some of their higher ups in Washington are involved in this, too. My only hope is that they think I'm still working with them."

"What about Clark? His family hasn't heard from him in days. Have they gotten to him?"

"It's possible. Anything is possible. He's considered a weak link. Expendable at this point. But, Gallagher, listen … did you get the key?"

"I was waiting for you to mention that. Yes, it came two days ago. I'm assuming it doesn't mean I just won a new car."

"It's the spare key to my car. You know it—the black Acura. I'm going to leave the car in a parking lot near the Metrorail Station near my house in the morning. I do that whenever we have meetings at the Pentagon, and we have one scheduled tomorrow. I'll take the train into the city. Just after dark, go to the parking lot near the entrance on Q Street and pick up the car. The tapes will be in my glove compartment. Just drive it right out of Washington, all the way to Boston if you like. But somehow, get those tapes to an FBI office or an agent you can trust."

"Why after dark? Can't I just pick it up during the day?"

"No ...too risky. The daytime attendant knows me and will see me drop the car off. She leaves at five o'clock. The lot is unattended at night. You don't want to blow this by getting picked up for stealing a car."

Her voice was frantic, almost pleading with him now. "Gallagher ... you've got to be here tomorrow. I don't know how many more days I can last before they figure me out. When they do, my life is over. Then, for sure, they'll come after you."

The phone suddenly clicked. Silence. He had more questions, but she was gone. Had she hung up abruptly because someone was there? Had her conversation been overheard? Had she been discovered? Had danger arrived before he could help her? He didn't dare call back; a call from him might put her in further jeopardy.

Her phone call disturbed him, to say the least. His vivid image of a sexy, sensuous, and confident woman was now replaced with that of the frightened, desperate person with whom he had just spoken. She hadn't merely asked for his help, she begged for it. He knew he had to act. To sit back and wait for something else to happen would only invite disaster. There was no way he could avoid the trip to Washington tomorrow. He had to help her.

Gallagher reached into his pants pocket and removed the key he had carried for the past few days. He rubbed his fingers over it, thinking of all of the possibilities the key represented. Was this a chance to end a conspiracy of government officials that threatened our national security? To save a woman who now risked her life to uncover the truth? To finally understand the motives behind the car bombing that took the life of Jennifer Clark—the innocent victim who made a simple decision that changed everything?

Jennifer could have asked her husband to move his car that Saturday morning. Instead, she grabbed his key chain from the kitchen counter, walked out to the driveway, and placed a key into the ignition. And then, the car blew up.

Gallagher continued to stare at the key in his hand. He felt a sudden chill. Was he walking into a trap? Did the key represent hope or an invitation to a deadly catastrophe? How could he be sure?

His thoughts flashed back to his meeting with Dougie Mannion, his short-statured friend who had referred him to an expert in explosives. Gallagher's plans suddenly took on a totally new dimension. Before he stepped on a plane to Washington, a critical call was necessary—one that could ultimately save his life.

Gallagher needed to reach Chuck Cumming, the man who operated a fireworks store in New Hampshire and the man who could tell him everything he needed to know about car bombs.

Chapter Thirty-Eight

Gallagher was on a tight schedule. He had to drive up to Salem, New Hampshire, and still get back to Logan International Airport in Boston in time for a three o'clock flight to Washington D.C. His mind buzzed with wild scenarios. Rebecca Johnson's plea sounded sincere and reasonable. If the plot to sell government secrets was as widespread as she described, she had no other choice. She had to seek help from an outside source. With the knowledge he already possessed, Gallagher represented her only viable option.

But what if her story was all a scam, a ploy to draw him in and then simply eliminate the person who had discovered the method by which information was being transferred to the North Koreans? How would he know? The answer had become obvious. If the key started her car, and he drove safely away with the evidence, Rebecca Johnson would be vindicated, perhaps even considered a hero for risking her life to prevent any further treason against the United States. If the key set off an explosion, Gallagher would have certainly investigated his last case.

"You have arrived at your destination," said the woman's voice from the GPS system. Gallagher turned into the parking lot of the strip mall and immediately noticed a red and yellow sign, Granite Fireworks, on the second store on the left. He walked into the store, and a young clerk greeted him at the register, "Morning. Can I help you find anything?"

"I'm looking for Chuck."

"He's in the workshop in the back. Straight down this aisle. The door is open."

Gallagher got to the doorway and looked into the room. Colorful boxes marked "Spinners," "Sparklers," and "Roman Candles" were stacked against the walls. A long wooden table was on the right side of the room with a four-foot fluorescent light fixture hanging above it. A man leaned over the table packaging an order of three boxes that were labeled "Aerial Arsenal Shell Kit." He looked to be about forty years old. He had tousled, brown hair, but a neatly trimmed beard, and wore jeans and a dark-blue sweatshirt. He glanced up at Gallagher, "Yes, what can I do for you?"

"My name's Gallagher. I'm a friend of Dougie Mannion."

"Who's Dougie Mannion? Am I supposed to know him?" he shot back.

"He said I should tell you that he remembers Bernadette."

Cumming's mouth dropped slightly open. He stared off to the side of the room for a few seconds. His shoulders slumped and he appeared detached from the scene as if absorbed in a painful flashback. Then he seemed to bounce back to reality. He looked over at Gallagher again. "Poor Dougie. He's doin' some hard time right now. How many more years left for him?"

"About five."

"That's rough. He's a good guy. He just got messed up with drugs and did some stupid things. Have you seen him lately? Is he alright?"

"I saw him about a week ago. You know Dougie...he'll tough it out. We're all pulling for him." Gallagher's curiosity, however, had gotten the best of him. "Do you mind me asking? Who's Bernadette?"

Cumming paused briefly as if considering whether he wanted to answer this question. He swallowed once, then stammered slightly while he seemed to search for the right words. Gallagher couldn't pick up what he said. Then Cumming came back with a question of his own. "Ever have a special woman? A once-in-a-lifetime woman?"

"Yes," said Gallagher soberly.   "In fact, I've got one of those now." His thoughts shifted to Kate. Here he was, pursuing another wild theory that may have put his life on the line. Had his selfish compulsions driven a permanent wedge between them? Would she ever come back to him when this case was over?

"Don't let her get away, man…don't let her get away. You'll spend the rest of your life wondering why you did."

"That's good advice. I'll try to remember it."

Gallagher didn't pursue the subject, recognizing that he may have brought up an uncomfortable matter that didn't deserve further elaboration. Cumming turned away from the table, walked over to the door, and closed it gently. He wanted whatever level of privacy the workshop could offer. He motioned toward a chair on the side of the table. "Have a seat. Tell me what I can do for you."

"I'm a private investigator. I need some information for a case I'm working on. My client's sister was killed by a bomb that was placed in her husband's car a couple of months ago."

Gallagher had garnered all of Cumming's attention.   "Killed? Whew!" he exclaimed as he exhaled deeply.

"Yes, her husband may have arranged it or possibly rigged it himself. To complicate matters a bit more, I'm leaving this afternoon to pick up a car in Washington. It's related to the same murder case. I want to know how I can tell if there's a surprise waiting for me under the hood"

"Pretty heavy stuff!" Cumming said. He paused for a few seconds, obviously trying to absorb the ramifications of Gallagher's story. He nodded his head slowly and then responded with a confident voice that indicated the breadth of his experience in these matters. "As far as the car in Washington, it's not easy. You have to hope they were a little sloppy and maybe left a few pieces of wire or tape that fell under the hood. The hood release is usually booby-trapped to set off the bomb. So maybe they didn't close the hood all the way, hoping to avoid settin' it off when the hood slammed down. But, other than that, it's almost impossible to tell."

Cumming's knowledge of this underworld topic was frighteningly acute. He went on to explain the various types of car bombs—the materials they were made from and how they were detonated. He described in detail the manner in which a few inches of thin wire were attached to the ignition coil and then extended to blasting caps that were usually tied to a few sticks of dynamite. When a key was inserted into the ignition and turned, the heat from the ignition coil spread through the wire and triggered the blasting caps to fire. The resulting explosion caused the gasoline tank to erupt in flames, rapidly killing the occupants of the car.

"The person setting the bomb has more options," Cumming said. "The key gets you into the car ... you turn the key ... nothing happens, and you feel safe. But they can load up the area under the hood with explosives not tied to the ignition. Then, they can activate the bomb from a short distance away with a remote control device or even a cell phone. And the car could be rigged with a motion sensor that can activate the bomb when you slam the door or try to open the trunk. So you gotta be careful. Most of the time, though, they don't wanna be in the area when the thing goes off. Why risk being seen? Better to be somewhere else and have an alibi."

"What about the sister of my client? Could her husband have set up the bomb in his own car the night before she got into it?"

"Sure, if he knew what he was doin'. Doesn't take that long if you have the right materials. And it's not a noisy job. If she was a sound sleeper, she wouldn't have heard a thing. But I'll tell you right now, unless you come up with some proof that he bought the stuff or someone saw him riggin' it, you'll never get this guy. That's the beauty of a car bomb. The evidence blows up with the victim."

Cumming's matter-of-fact approach to such lurid crimes was both impressive and unsettling at the same time. Gallagher didn't push for details about his first-hand experience in these felonious matters. He was certain, however, that his friend Dougie had frequently tapped this source of expertise while developing his specialty as an arsonist for hire.

They spoke for another twenty minutes as Cumming provided a complete primer on the science and art of configuring a car bomb. These were more instructions than Gallagher would ever need, but fascinating just the same.

On his drive to the airport, Gallagher tried to assimilate all of the information he had learned from Chuck Cumming. He knew that, ultimately, his decision to place the key into the ignition of Rebecca Johnson's car would be a matter of instinct and trust. Was she telling the truth? If he didn't offer to help, would his life be at risk from agents he could not identify but feared what he knew?

He had packed his gun in a small travel bag to be checked in with the luggage. This situation had become very complicated—completely unpredictable with the distinct possibility of a deadly outcome. *I don't know what's waiting for me in Washington. I'd better be ready.*

Chapter Thirty-Nine

The flight was uneventful. He tried to sleep, but even the intent to do so bordered on the absurd. *How could you think of taking a nap when so much is at stake?* He picked up his travel bag at the baggage claim area, hailed a cab, and was headed toward Dupont Circle by five o'clock.

Darkness had set in by the time his cab arrived at the Q Street entrance to the Metrorail. Rush hour traffic had made the ride take more time than he had expected. It was nearly six o'clock when he stepped out of the cab. He walked around the area for a few minutes for no particular reason other than to waste a little time. Besides, he hadn't had anything to eat since his late-morning breakfast. His eyes lit up when he saw the Starbucks coffee shop on the corner of Connecticut Avenue. He was in no hurry—this was the perfect place to camp out for a while until most of the commuters had left the area.

By seven-thirty, he was ready to make a move. He walked out of the coffee shop and turned left on Q Street. It had rained earlier in the day, and the sky was still cloudy and dark. The wet pavement and lack of moonlight made the night seem even darker. He walked almost two blocks down the street to an outdoor parking lot that was now nearly empty.

A quick count showed fewer than fifteen cars remaining. In the rear of the lot he could see a black Acura sedan that was parked facing away from the street. Having spent so much time following it on his previous trips to Washington D.C., he had no trouble verifying that this car belonged to Rebecca Johnson. There were no other cars parked to either side.

He opened the zipper of his coat and adjusted the shoulder strap of his holster. His .38 S & W revolver was in its customary accessible location in front of his left armpit. *Just in case. I want to be ready for anything I run into.*

As he walked slowly toward the car, his eyes gathered in the entire scene in front and around him. He was alone in the parking lot. In fact, the place was eerily quiet. Today's rain had been light, and the dry asphalt underneath some of the cars indicated which ones had been left since the early morning. He took notice of the fact that this was true of the surface below the black Acura. So far, Rebecca's story was holding up—she had planned to leave the car and take an early train to the Pentagon.

Gallagher approached the car cautiously. He walked all around the perimeter looking for any signs that someone had tampered with the vehicle. The hood was not ajar. He pulled a small flashlight out of his pocket, bent down, and shined it underneath the car, studying the asphalt surface for pieces of wire, tape or any debris that could be considered suspicious. Nothing but pebbles and the torn piece of a Hershey bar wrapper. He peered inside through the side windows. The seats and floor were clean and empty. Still, he was not totally satisfied that he could enter the car safely.

He stood up and took the key out of his pocket. He thought of opening the trunk to search for any bomb paraphernalia that could be hidden out of sight, but quickly discarded that idea. The vibration of opening the trunk could detonate a device located in the rear of the car. *That wouldn't be very smart,* he chastised himself.

Gallagher was convinced that he just needed to check one more area before he put an end to his search. The longer he crawled around this car like a car thief, the more he might attract attention and have to face the police. He got down on one knee and then rolled over onto his back. He shimmied his way under the front of the car and tilted his head and the small flashlight upward to inspect as much of the engine as could be seen. It was tough—but no sign of dynamite, blasting caps, tape, or loose wiring.

Relatively confident that the car was free of explosives, he wriggled out from under the front bumper, got up on one knee, and began to stand up. He was startled by a low, almost raspy voice that came from a figure that had suddenly appeared and now stood over him. The voice had the seductive, sultry tone that he recognized so well from his first encounter in the bar at the Station Grill in Union Station—the voice of Rebecca Johnson.

"Looking for something, Gallagher?" she said with a sarcastic sneer.

"Becky," he replied, as he continued to get up. "I didn't expect to see—"

His words were harshly interrupted by a powerful force that came crashing down on the back of his head. He reeled backward and down to the ground. His head throbbed with pain. He could hardly focus his eyes as everything appeared in double or triple images.

He rolled onto his back, instinctively reaching for his gun. But his reaction time had been grossly slowed by the impact of the blow to his head. He was way too late. He felt his gun being pulled from the holster.

He was now disarmed—defenseless and vulnerable to the whims of his attackers. Gallagher knew that Rebecca had been in front of him, but she must have had an accomplice to the rear. Who was it? Who was her partner, the person that helped to set up this violent ambush?

His trust in her had clearly been misplaced. The deadly trap he had tried to avoid within the car was really the car itself, positioned and waiting for him to drop his guard. *How could I be so stupid? To let this bitch get the best of me!*

Now flat on his back, he looked up at her. His head continued pounding with almost deafening pulsations. Blood flowed from his scalp wound. He could feel the wetness of the accumulating red puddle that gathered around the back of his head. His eyes squinted tightly to help bring her into view.

He wanted to see her and to better understand this woman who had so viciously and cleverly arranged his demise. How different she looked—the beautiful face with those striking, sensuous features had been replaced with this harsh, angry countenance that bore the fury and rage of the person behind it.

She lifted a gun and pointed the barrel directly at him. She said nothing. Only seconds had passed, but it seemed like hours since he had crawled out from under the hood of the car. His body seemed powerless to act—almost paralyzed by the crushing blow that had forced him to the ground.

He closed his eyes, expecting the end to occur at any instant. His thoughts flashed to Kate, his parents, his friends. Would they ever know what happened? Would anyone learn the truth about this scheming, diabolical woman? The woman who was about to snuff out his life?

A gunshot rang out. It was loud and echoed throughout the parking lot. But his body didn't move—no additional pain. *Was this how death felt?*

He struggled to open his eyes. He heard a man shouting but could not understand what he was saying. He looked up at Rebecca Johnson. She was falling violently in a backward direction. Her face became oddly twisted and contorted as if she were suddenly in excruciating pain. She still held the gun in her right hand. He feared that she would pull the trigger and he would be struck with a random shot.

Then another loud sound reverberated through the air. Her body jerked sharply to the right. The gun seemed to fly from her flailing hand, propelled by a force that overwhelmed her. She tried to resist and keep her balance. But it was no use. Rebecca's body slowly slumped down along the side of the car until it finally collapsed into a crumpled heap on the pavement beside him.

Gallagher turned his head in order to see what had just happened. An ever-widening stream of blood flowed from Rebecca's forehead and ran down over her eyebrows and across her face. Her left hand made a futile attempt to clutch at her chest where another dark, wet stain was enlarging. Within seconds the hand fell softly to her side. Her chest was unmoving. Her mouth sagged open. Rebecca Johnson was dead.

Gallagher heard footsteps running toward him—the rapid clicking of leather heels against the wet asphalt made it seem like an army approaching. The sounds of men yelling became a thunderous roar. Someone shouted, "Keep your hands above your head."

He tried to remain alert and to fathom the horrific events of the past few seconds. But his brain was in a state of shock, and he could not fight the light-headed feeling that overcame him.

Gallagher closed his eyes and drifted off into unconsciousness.

Chapter Forty

"This fuckin' guy is nowhere to be found. He's not home; he's never in his office. Maybe someone else got in on this gig and already took him out." Lou Wilson was clearly frustrated, and he was getting antsy. He had little patience for this waiting game.

"I thought we had the bastard two weeks ago," chimed in Ben. "It was a perfect setup."

"Perfect? Did you say perfect? You asshole! You almost put us in the slammer by being so trigger happy! That guy you shot didn't even look like our mark." Lou stood by the window of the second-floor motel room looking down at the traffic buzzing up Route 95 in Newton. He sipped from a cup of black coffee and continued facing the window even though he directed his verbal barbs at his partner who was lying on a bed.

Ben rolled over on the bed and took his eyes off the television. "Yeah, but what else did you want me to do? Once he saw us, he could have ID'd us to the police. I thought he was making a move. I had to take him out. You're the one that's always preachin' 'No living witnesses.'"

"The guy was a burglar!" Lou bellowed. "What's he gonna do, call the police and say, 'I was robbing this office and two guys walked in on me. Would you like their description so you can arrest them?' You are

155

fuckin' unbelievable!" He had become totally fed up with his partner's impulsive actions.

"Hey, Lou. I'm gettin' sick of telling you I'm sorry," Ben challenged. He stood up, took an aggressive stance and stared fiercely at the source of the verbal assault. His cut-off tee shirt allowed him to display his powerful arms that flexed repeatedly when he became angry, demonstrating his potential for physical retaliation. "It happened ... now it's over ... you gotta deal with it. At least we came out of it with almost a thousand bucks for our trouble. The guy's wallet was loaded."

Lou took notice of his partner's agitated state and immediately toned down his insulting rhetoric. "Alright ... alright. Forget it! Just our luck it was that Fleming guy instead of Gallagher. It would have been sweet to catch him late at the office with nobody around on our first try. Then all we had to do was find the wife. Take her out and collect our thirty grand. Now we can't locate either one of them. I don't get it."

"How much longer are we gonna give this? I'm gettin' sick of hangin' around here with no action. We're just eatin' up our profits on motel bills. I hate this god-damned place."

"Another week, maybe ten days. We'll leave when I decide it's time. Look, we had to lay low for a while. His office was crawling with cops after that night. Makes me wonder, though, there must be something valuable in that office or else that guy wouldn't have been there. We might have missed our chance in more ways than one."

"Nah, all I saw was a bunch of papers. This whole deal may not be worth the trouble we're goin' through. I'd be happy if we just forgot it and got the hell outta' here."

"Do you know what you're sayin'? The guy that hired us isn't going to be happy if we go home empty handed. Something tells me he's backed with a lot of muscle. You know, the kind of guy who never wants to be double-crossed. No, Ben, we better finish this job or else we could be sorry."

Lou continued staring out the window, running contingency plans through his mind. *Eventually, this guy has to show his face, and when he does, we won't waste any time taking him out. If we have to break into his house and be there waiting for him, we'll do it. Sooner or later, he's got to show up. Then we're on our way and no one knows what hit him.*

Chapter Forty-One

At least the throbbing in Gallagher's head had diminished. He just felt weak and hungry. He couldn't remember the last time he tasted food. In fact, there seemed to be a lot he couldn't remember. *How long have I been lying here? In fact, where am I? This strange, light-headed feeling... are they pumping Valium into me?*

He opened his eyes and saw clear plastic tubing leading out of his left arm and coursing upward to a collapsing, half-empty bag hanging from an intravenous pole. *Guess I'm getting lunch, but I'd rather have something I could chew.* He turned his head to the right. A man with wavy, brown hair was sitting on a chair next to his bed. His jaw jutted slightly forward as he smiled and began speaking in a gentle, deep voice, "Glad you finally decided to wake up. Thought you were going to sleep for a few more days."

Gallagher delayed for a few seconds, trying to remember if he had ever seen this face before. His memory drew a blank. "Mind if I ask you a few questions?"

"Not at all," the man said. Then he laughed softly and added, "That's why I'm here. I'll bet you've got a lot of questions after everything you've been through."

"Well, for openers, who the hell are you and where am I?"

"I'm Dom Melone, Department of Defense Investigations Unit. You're in the Walter Reed Medical Center. It's less than five miles from

Dupont Circle. We brought you here in an ambulance right after that commotion the other night. How's your head feeling? The doctors said you had quite a concussion."

"Guess I'll be alright." It was not his head right now that concerned him—he wanted something to eat. He felt his stomach growling. He was dying of thirst, beyond the point of parched. "Do they have any food in this place, or am I just on the liquid diet that comes from that bag up there?"

Melone laughed a little louder. "Oh, that tells me you are feeling better!" He stood up and pressed a red rubber button attached to a long cord on the side of the bed. A nurse promptly came into the room. "Mr. Gallagher would like something to eat. Can you bring him a little food?"

The nurse smiled, "Welcome back to the real world. I'll be right back with some breakfast."

"I'll have a large coffee with that," prompted Gallagher.

She shook her head and wagged her finger, playfully admonishing him. "Uh, uh, sorry …no caffeine with that big bump on your head and the medication you're taking. You'll have to wait until the doctor says it's okay. I'll bring some orange juice instead."

"Great," Gallagher moaned. "I thought the government had abolished the practice of torturing its prisoners." She walked away laughing, putting him on notice that his request was getting no sympathy from her. *How did I get so lucky to have Nurse Ratched taking care of me?*

Melone sat down and directed his attention toward Gallagher again. "Would you like to get back to your questions?"

"Yes, in fact I would. Tell me what happened the other night. My mind is a bit foggy after the point where I crawled out from under the car and someone smashed the back of my head. Who shot Rebecca Johnson?"

"One of my agents, a former Army marksman. Doesn't miss."

"I noticed."

"Too bad he didn't shoot before you got walloped in the back of your head, but we had to wait to see how all of this played out. We've been watching you since you met with Becky in the bar at Union Station.

We weren't sure if you were in on their scheme. Once they attacked you, we knew we had to act or you would have been a goner."

"Who was with her?"

"Tom Manzelli, Deputy Director of the CIA."

"Is he dead, too?"

"No. He surrendered to us in the parking lot. When he saw Becky hit the ground, he knew we meant business. He's been talking to us for the past three days. It makes sense for him to try to plead out on this. We caught them red-handed. Most of what we know today has come from Manzelli."

"I still don't get it. How did you figure out what was happening?"

"We had been tracking Bill Clark for quite some time, but nothing came out of it. We began to think that he was just a victim and that his wife had been killed and the poor guy had fallen under suspicion without good reason."

"What made you change your mind?"

"Well, he began spending a considerable amount of time in Sterling at the girlfriend's house. We did a lot of checking. We turned up witnesses who said that Clark had been visiting her even before his wife was killed. So much for the grieving widower saga."

Gallagher nodded his head in agreement and then added, "Jennifer Clark's sister had that one pegged all along."

"We also found out that the girlfriend had no financial resources and no real job. How could she buy that condo and live such an expensive lifestyle? Also, she was making small cash deposits into her bank account on a regular basis. If the money was coming from Clark, we knew he couldn't afford it on the salary he was making. He had to be getting extra money from another source. You know the old story: follow the money."

"Then what?" asked Gallagher, eager to get more of the details.

"If Clark was selling classified information, we figured he would try to avoid any meetings with his contacts and never use his own phone to call them. He wouldn't want to leave a trail with phone records that were in his name. But he had to make calls from somewhere. Fortunately for us, he got a bit sloppy."

Gallagher sat up in his bed. This story was getting more interesting by the minute.

Melone continued. "We put a tap on the girlfriend's phone and got copies of her cell-phone records. Sure enough, the same numbers kept popping up. One of the numbers he called repeatedly belonged to Rebecca Johnson. That really shocked us. And his calls to her started before his wife was killed."

"You mean she was in on the car bombing that killed Jennifer Clark?"

"Yes ... Manzelli confirmed it. Becky arranged the whole thing."

Gallagher was in disbelief. "But she loved that woman. Had an affair with her for a few months. How could she do that?"

Melone smiled and shook his head. "If Becky Johnson went to Hollywood, she'd win an Academy Award. She could lie her way out of any situation. We are just beginning to understand the depths of her deception. When Becky was sent up to Boston to spy on Clark and infiltrate his house, she figured out what Clark was up to. She knew he had to be collecting plenty of cash for trading information to the North Koreans and wanted to get in on the take."

"So, money was her motive."

"Yes. Isn't it always part of the equation? She also found out about his mistress. She may have gotten that information by getting close to his wife. Clark was thinking of asking Jennifer for a divorce, but was hesitant to be forced to split all their assets. Becky offered him a way to get out of the marriage without losing anything. In exchange, she became his partner. Even upped the ante and pushed for delivering more classified information to obtain greater payoffs. She was ruthless."

"So her story about being involved with the espionage ring and the sale of information to the North Koreans was true after all. Why did she risk telling me?" asked Gallagher, puzzled by the way this story was unfolding.

"She was going to do away with you anyway. It didn't matter. You had already discovered their method of passing the information. But, you have to admit, she made herself sound contrite and believable. Her story convinced you to come back to Washington where she could eliminate you."

The nurse came back with his breakfast—two scrambled eggs, hash brown potatoes, two pieces of toast, and a glass of orange juice.

He was famished and began devouring the food. Melone continued providing the details as Gallagher listened attentively in between bites. "By the way," said Melone, "that was some pretty good detective work you did to connect the priest to their plans. Our agents totally missed that."

Gallagher appreciated the compliment, but chose to go on with another question. "What's going to happen to the Monsignor?"

"He's just a poor, misguided individual who tried to save his parish and really didn't understand the details about the sensitive nature of the information he was transporting. The code-breaking formulas were a form of mathematics completely out of his league, and he probably never looked at them. My guess is that the courts will go pretty easy on him. But the bottom line is that it was an act of treason, so he will have to do some jail time."

"What about Bill Clark? I spoke to his sister-in-law. His family hadn't heard from him in a few days."

"Yes, there's a good reason for that. He's dead."

"Becky again?"

"Yes. Manzelli told us where we could find his body. Becky arranged to meet him, ostensibly for a payoff from the latest transaction. She was afraid he might talk someday and implicate her. She had already collected enough money to run off to some exotic island and live the life of a rich, retired woman."

"How did they get their money? They must have had a contact here in the U.S."

"You're right. We're still working on that. But we have arrested the diamond merchant who was living with her."

"Diamond merchant? I thought he was a corporate lawyer."

Melone couldn't contain his laughter. "Sounds like another one of Becky's stories! Part of the payoffs they received was in the form of smuggled diamonds. Becky met up with this guy, moved in with him, and worked out a system where he laundered the smuggled diamonds on the black market and gave her the cash. Yes, Becky had it all figured out. She knew all the angles."

That's the last time I'll assume I know someone's identity based on their stereotypical appearance. Sometimes, Gallagher, you are an idiot!

The bout of self-flagellation was short-lived. Dozens of questions were popping into Gallagher's head. "But why did she need Manzelli? Didn't that just give her another person to split the profits with?"

"She needed Manzelli to misdirect the rest of the investigators, and to keep them away from Clark and looking at other sources for the leaks. Her plan was working beautifully. She even had us fooled. And then, you came on the scene. You eventually forced her hand and brought her out into the open."

"That just leaves one final question. Who sent the guy that was found dead in my office?"

"Oh, yes ... Mark Fleming. He was a former CIA agent who left the Agency about ten years ago. Becky must have kept in touch with him and hired him to break into your office."

"What was he looking for?"

"She had to be sure you didn't have any written files or reports on your findings about Clark or anything that could implicate her. Manzelli told us she was worried about you. She thought you might know more than you were letting on—sort of an unknown wild card. When Fleming didn't get back to her the next day, she and Manzelli panicked. At first, she thought you might have killed him when you found him rummaging through the office. She had to wait a few days until the story broke in the news. Once she knew Fleming was dead, she tried to lure you back to Washington."

"So who killed Fleming?"

"That's a question we still haven't been able to answer. Maybe he brought somebody along with him and something happened. We don't know. Eventually, we'll find out. We usually do."

"And Clark's mistress? Does she have any culpability in all of this?"

"Oh, Lindsay? Nice looking babe, but very naïve. She'll probably come out of this unscathed. She'll have to forfeit the condo and her car since they were purchased with illegal money. But I doubt that she'll be indicted if she cooperates with the investigators and tells them everything she knows."

Gallagher finished his glass of orange juice and heaved a big sigh. "So I guess that pretty much wraps up this case. You've got to let me know if you learn anything more about the person who shot Mark Fleming. That's the one loose end that still bothers me."

"I can understand your concern. After your meeting with Becky at Union Station, we kept a tail on you when you got back to Massachusetts. But you went home that night, not to your office. So Fleming's death is a mystery to us, too."

"Wish you'd tell that to Detective Phillips in Boston Homicide. He's been pestering me since it happened."

Melone laughed again. "Don't worry. We'll tell him to get off your back. We've kept this story away from the media and the local police until we had the facts and knew all of the players. We're not quite done yet, but we're awfully close." His calm demeanor was reassuring. Gallagher was sure that Melone's methodical approach to this probe and the collection of federal investigators at his disposal would ultimately provide answers to these remaining questions.

Melone stood up and put on the sport coat that had been draped over the back of his chair. He adjusted his tie and gave Gallagher a knowing look—almost half a smile. He looked as though he had one last surprise for his new friend with the bandage wrapped around his head.

"By the way, Gallagher, there's something else you should know."

"Haven't you hit me with enough for one day?"

Melone chuckled. "We wondered why you were crawling around looking under the car with a flashlight. So after the ambulance took you here, we called in the bomb squad to check it out. Good thing you never tried to start that car. It was loaded with explosives."

Melone walked to the door of the hospital room and gave him a little wave. "Take care of yourself, Gallagher. I'll be in touch with you."

Gallagher sat back in his bed, almost stunned by the magnitude of Melone's disclosures in the past hour. Rebecca Johnson, the woman Jennifer Clark had known as her lover, Marcie Williams, had proven to be one of the most resourceful criminals he had ever known. She was shrewd and brilliant—willing to exhaust all means to accomplish her goals. But, in the end, her talent was wasted. She never secured her place in the fantasyland she so wistfully described.

Now, however, it was time for Gallagher to think about going home. To put all of this behind him and begin to resolve the important issues in his life. Had the breach in his marriage become irreconcilable? Would he be able to get back together with Kate? Could he finally give up a career that seemed plagued with more danger and occupational hazards than should be tolerated?

And the hospital? Keep this story away from Kate for the present time. The news of another attack on his life would be too unsettling and only reinforce her persistent worries about his safety. Better to explain what happened in person and reassure her that this case was over.

Gallagher planned to be discharged from the hospital on the following day and return to Boston on a late afternoon flight. He considered himself fortunate that his injuries were not permanent. The doctors had told him they expected him to make a full recovery.

Chapter Forty-Two

The phone rang in Brewster, Massachusetts. Kate picked up the handset and stood by the large picture window in the living room. It was a cold but clear day, and in the distance across Cape Cod Bay she could see the 252-foot high Pilgrim Monument in Provincetown—the tallest all-granite structure in the United States.

"Hey, it's me again," Gallagher said softly.

The sound of his voice sparked an immediate reaction. "I haven't heard from you in days. Are you all right?"

"Oh, I'm fine. I'm catching a plane late this afternoon. I should be home by nine or so."

"Was that a hesitation I noticed? Are you sure everything is okay?"

He should have known he couldn't fool her—she knew him like a book. "Just a little bump on my head. Nothing to worry about," he said, trying to brush off the significance of his injuries.

"You're lying."

"Not me."

"You're insufferable."

"Isn't that why you love me so much?"

"Cut it out! Just tell me…where are you?"

"Washington."

"Again?"

165

"Yeah, funny how I keep coming back here."

"Did you find your missing woman?"

"Yes."

"Get her back to where she belongs?"

He paused again. This was not the time for any specifics about the events of the past few weeks. "Oh yeah...she's right where she belongs."

"And what's next?" He could feel the sarcasm biting at him through the phone.

Now he got serious. He searched for the right combination of words but settled for the basics. "Kate...will you come back?"

There was silence and a painful wait. "I don't know. It's complicated."

"I need you."

"But you don't understand what I need."

"I'll stop. Things will be different."

"You said that the last time. What happens when you get a call about another missing woman? You'll drop everything and go running off again."

"I won't."

She went back to his earlier story. "A little bump in the head? I don't think so. Someone probably tried to kill you."

He ignored her correct assumption and kept pushing. "You know we love each other."

"Love isn't enough. There's a whole package you can't see. I need a husband who comes home every night to a safe, happy place to be a father to his children. What will I say to our kids? Daddy had to chase some bad guys today. Let's say a prayer and hope he comes home alive?"

"I'll give it up."

"You might say that, but you don't mean it."

She stared out the window. Like the monument off in the distance, she could never quite reach him—he'd never understand. Her eyes welled up with tears. She could hardly get the words out. "I have to think ... bye." The phone clicked. She was gone.

*   *   *

Gallagher's mind was whirling. His thoughts flashed back to the fireworks store in Salem, New Hampshire. *Don't let her get away, man. Don't let her get away. You'll spend the rest of your life wondering why you did.*

In his heart, he knew it was too late. He felt as though his life would never be the same again.

Chapter Forty-Three

Two nights earlier they had executed the first part of their plan. At three o'clock in the morning, Ben Harris slipped a razor sharp Italian stiletto blade under the telephone wires at the side of the ranch style house. One quick slice severed the line and immediately activated the burglar alarm. A loud horn blared throughout the house and neighborhood.

Lou Wilson had positioned himself strategically at the rear entrance off the deck. As soon as the alarm sounded, he placed a grooved flat key into the lock of the back door and hit it hard with a hammer. This move, known as lock bumping—a great technique he had learned in his days as a two-bit burglar—worked, and within seconds he was inside the house and swiftly made his way to the entryway closet at the side of the living room. He opened the closet, reached up to the control box, and cut the wires leading to the alarm horn. Then, he smashed the control box and dismantled the battery back-up.

The deafening reverberation of the alarm was replaced by stillness. The only sound Lou could hear was his own rapid breathing that resulted from his wild dash into the house and assault on the contents of the closet. The entire exercise had taken less than thirty seconds.

He rushed over to the front window and peered across the wide cul-de-sac at two similar ranch-style homes. No lights. No doors opening. His assumption had been correct—the frequency of false alarms in today's environment had numbed the suspicions of the neighbors. By disconnecting the horn so quickly, he had kept the disturbance to a minimum. Perhaps no one even heard it.

Lou had no fear that the police would be dispatched to investigate the break-in. Ben had eliminated that possibility by cutting the telephone line, precluding the transmission of an alert to the alarm company and then to the police.

The house remained in darkness. Ben walked in through the broken back door and stumbled over a chair in the small dining area next to the kitchen. "Lou!" he called.

"Over here, by the front door. Keep it down."

"Anybody see us?" he whispered.

Lou continued staring out the window, never looking back toward his clumsy partner. "Don't think so. Seems like no one got up in those houses across the road. Not one light went on. I think we're home free."

Ben walked in closer. Lou could sense him gawking over his shoulder, trying to add his eyes to the lookout team. "You're right," Ben said. "No lights. Looks like we're all set."

These two were veterans of such break-ins. They were experienced, calculating, and willing to take chances, and they were loaded with knowledge about alarms and security systems. They knew enough to be ready to bolt at the hint of discovery.

"Now you see why I went to that realtor's open house yesterday. Five of these condos are on the market. I walked all around, opening doors until I figured out where the alarm control box was located. They build all of these places the same way, like with a cookie cutter. Makes it easy if you want to get to that alarm."

"Now what?"

"We sit tight and wait. No more of those hotel bills that had you so worried. We just figured out the perfect way to cut our overhead."

"Sweet."

"And when this guy walks in the door, he's in for the surprise of his life."

"What about the car?"

Lou continued his surveillance operation, carefully studying the two houses across the street. "Let's wait a few more minutes to make sure the neighbors are sleeping tight. Then bring it around and put it in the garage so it's off the street. I'll disconnect the automatic opener. When he comes back, we'll force him to use the front door."

"Nice."

"Hey ... whattya expect?" Lou proclaimed with an air of bravado and turning toward his admiring accomplice. "When you work with me, I take care of all the plans and make all the arrangements. Your job is to make sure this guy doesn't walk out of here alive."

"No problem. You leave that to me," Ben chuckled. Then he broke out into an outright laugh—his thoughts evidently striking a very amusing chord. "Don't worry ... you leave that to me!"

Chapter Forty-Four

Man ... you look like crap!

Gallagher stared into the bathroom mirror of his hospital room. Four days in this place had left him looking pale and gaunt. The back of his head still ached from the crushing blow he had received in the parking lot. Fortunately, his memory had improved to the point where he was confident that his brain had not suffered permanent damage.

He got dressed and combed his hair, trying to cover the shaved bare spot at the back of his head where the emergency room doctor had placed the stitches. *That guy might have been a good doctor, but he'd make a lousy barber.*

The sound of someone entering the room interrupted his grousing. A woman's voice called his name. "Are you alright, Mr. Gallagher?" she asked.

"Yes, just getting ready to leave." He opened the door. The nurse he had referred to as "Nurse Ratched" was smiling at him. Her name tag read "Nancy, RN."

"Going back to Boston?" she asked.

His initial impression had been wrong—she wasn't so bad, after all. She just had to do a better job recognizing when a man craved a cup of coffee. "Yes. I've got a flight tonight at six."

"Your wife will be glad to see you."

"How did you know I'm married?"

"Saw the ring."

"Oh … yeah." He looked at the black and blue marks on the back of his left hand. "Probably noticed it when you were taping up the IV."

"Hey, when you're thirty-five and single, you always notice if there's a ring."

"I guess," he replied, trying to be pleasant and go along with her humor.

"So, you're a private detective? Must be pretty exciting at times."

"Exciting? Did you see the gash back here?" he asked as he pointed to the back of his head.

"Sorry, I didn't mean it that way."

"No problem. You're right. Some days do have their share of excitement."

"How's your head feeling?"

"Still hurts, but not as much as yesterday."

"Your meds are probably kicking in pretty well now. You'll need to keep taking them for another week or so," she said.

"Ibuprofen twice a day. Is that enough?"

"That should work. Don't worry, you'll feel better when you're home with your family. Any kids?"

"No, not yet. I haven't been married that long." *What is this? Another police inquisition?* he wondered.

"Well, you'll get a big welcome from your wife."

"Maybe."

"Uh oh, I didn't like the sound of that. Sounds like there could be a little trouble on the home front. I know all about that; I've been there."

Gallagher excused himself from any further conversation. She was nice enough, but a little too chatty to suit his mood. Besides, everything she said seemed to strike a nerve and echo of the pain in his life. He had no interest in hearing any details about her problems.

By two o'clock, he had signed all the necessary papers for his discharge and was on his way. Dom Melone had made arrangements for him to pick up his .38 revolver from the security office at the Pentagon. The rest of Melone's report had been disappointing—no new developments in the case involving Rebecca Johnson, Bill Clark, and Tom Manzelli.

Loose ends. He hated loose ends.

Why haven't they come up with one plausible theory about the shooting of Mark Fleming in my office? Should I call Kate again? My life seems to be one big screw-up. What am I going to do now?

He hailed a cab and headed to the airport. He couldn't get Kate off his mind.

Maybe she'll be there when I get home tonight.

Chapter Forty-Five

The trash was stacked in the back entryway. Camped out at Gallagher's house for the past three days, Lou Wilson and Ben Harris felt right at home by this time. They watched TV, drank all the coffee, and raided the kitchen cabinets, refrigerator, and freezer for any food that caught their interest. Rations were not the issue—the boring waiting game was what tested their mettle.

"I'm tellin' you, Lou. One more day and I'm outta here. If this guy doesn't show by tomorrow, count me out," said Ben.

Lou chose to ignore him. Instead, from his seat by the window, he continued to peer down the street to see if any cars had turned onto the road leading to the cul-de-sac. He had timed it precisely. A car turning left from the main road needed at least twenty seconds to get to the driveway. Plenty of time to douse the lights and get to their predetermined stations: Lou—shielded by the bedroom door—and Ben, hidden by the wall between the dining room and the kitchen. Both would have a direct line of sight to the front door. When Gallagher entered and closed the door, they would make their move. Even better if he walked in with his wife.

"Did you hear me, Lou? One more day..."

"Oh, shut up!" Lou yelled back. "I heard ya'."

"Hey!" Ben challenged, showing his dislike for being chastised like a whining child.

Lou, however, persisted with his reprimand. "Will you just chill out? Why don't you get some rest so you'll be able to stay awake when it's your turn over here?"

"I'm not tired, just bored with this whole deal. We're like sitting ducks here. The cops could come by anytime, and we'd be screwed. The longer we wait, the worse it gets."

"No reason for the cops to come. Nobody knows we're here. You just remember to keep these on." He held up a box of disposable rubber gloves. "No fingerprints. When we leave, they find one body, maybe two, and no evidence about who did it."

Lou went back to sentry duty. He stared out the window at the road leading up to the driveway, looking down occasionally and idly adjusting the silencer on his Glock 9mm automatic pistol. He knew his partner was just blowing smoke. He'd never leave without Lou's approval.

Lou had the perfect plan, but just one problem: *Where is this guy?*

Chapter Forty-Six

Four and a half days in Central Parking at Logan International Airport—one hundred and forty-four dollars. The bump on the back of his head felt worse. He drove through the Ted Williams Tunnel to the Mass Turnpike West, then Route 95 South to Needham. Within thirty minutes he was turning left on his street. *Good to be home.*

9:20 PM. He pulled into the driveway and pressed the automatic garage door opener. The door didn't lift. He tried again—nothing. The houses across the street had lights. *No power failure in the neighborhood.* He got out of the car and looked around. The house was in darkness. Not surprising, since he had turned off all the lights when he left for Washington. The garage door had never failed before. *What the hell is going on here?*

He had left his gun in the small travel bag he checked with the luggage. Now he reached into the car, unzipped the bag, and removed the gun from its steel security box. He slipped it into the right pocket of his jacket. *Just in case.*

He left the headlights of his car turned on, walked to the front door and fumbled to find the key. *I never come in this way.* He unlocked the dead-bolt, then the lock in the doorknob. He turned the knob and opened the door. Silence. The high-pitched whirr of the alarm system was missing.

Someone's been here! Kate? No … not without any lights on. He reached for his gun with his right hand.

He dove into the living room and squatted down by the couch. The beam of his headlights bounced off the garage door and dimly illuminated the room. For a few seconds, the room was still. Then suddenly, motion erupted all around him. The bedroom door opened. A tall, thin man emerged. Something in his right hand flashed in the light—a gun. Simultaneously, another much broader figure spun around the corner from the kitchen. The quiet "poof" of gunshots hit the couch in rapid succession.

Silencers! These guys are professionals! A hail of gunfire. The men were quick; Gallagher's response was quicker. The first shot from his .38 struck the tall man in the neck and dropped him like a stone. His body crashed to the floor.

As Gallagher turned to face the second man, his left arm went limp. He had been shot. Now bleeding profusely, the arm was dead weight. He lost his balance and stumbled out of his crouch. He fell onto his left side. The pain in his wounded arm seared through him. He aimed his gun at the attacker near the kitchen and fired. But his next two shots missed, as the large man retreated around the wall partition. Gallagher slithered forward—almost a crawl—to be in a better position to defend himself and have a clearer shot when the man showed himself again. In a heartbeat the large man reappeared, blasting away with his automatic weapon. But his aim was poor. He fired at Gallagher's previous location. Gallagher squeezed the trigger three times. The loud crack of gunfire reverberated through the house. A thunderous roar, "Aaargh!" came from the second attacker. *I probably got him twice!* The man fell backward and slammed into the kitchen cabinets.

Out of ammunition, Gallagher moved toward the body of the dead man near the bedroom door. He looked all around trying to locate the dead man's gun. He needed this weapon. The second man could still be alive and armed. Then he spotted it—a Glock automatic pistol— lying on the hardwood floor beyond the dead man's outstretched arm. Gallagher reached for the gun.

But he was too late. A sledgehammer punch hit him from behind and drove him down to the floor. He swiped for the gun but only succeeded in spinning it toward the center of the room, far from his grasp. He turned quickly to offer a defense from the physical attack. A broad, burly man stood over him—beads of perspiration billowed off his shaved head and blood dripped from his mouth. There were blood stains all over his shirt. *How is this guy able to stand up with two bullet holes in him?*

The bleeding man pounced down on Gallagher and grabbed him around the neck. His hands felt like the sides of a vise, and his grip was immensely powerful. Gallagher's eyes bulged. His face pounded with increasing pressure. He couldn't speak. No air. Desperate for a breath, he slammed his knee into the larger man's groin. He dug his fist into his side. Neither maneuver had any effect. The man continued to crush his throat. Gallagher felt his body getting limp—his life being squeezed away.

Someone screamed. The lights went on. Still no let up of the devastating clamp compressing his neck. Gallagher's resistance had evaporated. His heart rate became rapid—almost purposeless—no oxygen could get to his vital organs. His brain began drifting off into blankness.

Two shots fired—then a third. Gallagher hardly heard them. The death grip loosened. He gasped. A breath of air got in. He coughed again and again—hyperventilating—trying to suck in every waft—to bring life back to his oxygen-starved tissues.

The vicious clasp around his neck completely eased. The massive man, who had been kneeling and applying a stranglehold, now toppled forward on top of him.

Gallagher tried to push him off and roll to the side from under this squashing weight. But the pain in his shoulder, the paralysis of his left arm, and the weakness from excessive blood loss combined to prevent him from doing it alone. Police sirens sounded in the distance and grew closer. *Thank God someone called the police!*

He moved his head to the side and looked up. He expected to see a police officer or a neighbor who had intervened to rescue him from the near deadly attack. Instead, he saw a solitary figure—a woman— trembling and standing in the center of the room. The gun dropped from her hand. She rushed over to him.

The last thing he remembered was the horrified look on Kate's face.

Chapter Forty-Seven

Déjà vu all over again. Four days later, Dom Melone walked into Gallagher's hospital room. This time he was accompanied by a man in his early fifties—tall, about six foot one, with wavy, silver-gray hair and a mustache. He looked serious, and everything about him said "police."

"Hey, Melone," said Gallagher, sitting up in his bed. "We have to stop meeting in hospitals. I know a great bar in Revere ... the Driftwood. Next time, how 'bout we get together there and I'll buy you a drink?"

"I'd be happy to meet you somewhere else, but you're the one who keeps finding the trouble."

"You've got a point there, Melone. I'm gonna work on that."

"How's your arm?"

"The doctor says it'll be okay. No nerve damage. They repaired the muscle in the OR yesterday. I'll be in this sling for a week, then start my rehab."

"And, your neck?"

"Nothing broken."

"You're lucky to be alive. According to my count, that's four times in the last year."

"Guess it pays to be Irish."

"Or have a wife that can shoot straight."

"Yes, that always helps."

"We interviewed Kate two days ago," said Melone, now trying to skip past the humorous preludes.

"She told me all about it."

"Pretty special woman you've got there."

"You're not here just to tell me I've got a great wife. Isn't this the part where you and your quiet friend tell me what's been going on?"

"Oh, yes, excuse me. This is Scott Wayne, FBI, Boston office. He's in charge of the investigation from here on out."

"Investigation?"

"Yes. We're still trying to figure out why those two men wanted to kill you."

"You mean they weren't part of Rebecca Johnson's team?"

Scott Wayne stepped closer and spoke for the first time. He had a New York accent. *What's he doing in Boston?* "No, this had nothing to do with Rebecca Johnson. These guys were totally independent. For some reason, they targeted you."

"Who were they?"

"We ran their fingerprints and DNA. Their names were Lou Wilson and Ben Harris out of Chicago, both with long rap sheets. Wilson served time for breaking and entering and later for armed robbery. Harris did four years for assault with intent to murder. Word on the street is that his specialty was strangling his victims with his bare hands. Apparently got his jollies out of that."

"Yeah, tell me about it," Gallagher said and exhaled, reliving his recent experience with Harris's powerful grip on his neck.

"Both had mob connections, but none of our sources in Chicago know why they were in Boston. Do you?"

"No idea."

"They were apparently camped out at your place for a few days. They cut the wires to your alarm system and wore rubber gloves so they wouldn't leave any fingerprints around. They hid their car in your garage. The car had a set of phony Massachusetts plates. We found the Illinois plates in the trunk. They also had plenty of cash in their wallets. It was definitely a planned hit. Someone put a price on your head."

"Either one of them talk before they died?"

Wayne shook his head and smiled admiringly. "No. You blew a hole right through Wilson's carotid artery, and he died instantly. Good shot."

"I just reacted. I didn't have much time to think about it."

Wayne chuckled. Then he continued, "Harris ended up with five bullets in him … two from you and three from your wife. Took a lot to bring him down. He was a huge guy who would have been a good nose tackle for the Bears." Gallagher ignored the attempt at humor.

Melone interjected, "You might be interested in the results of the ballistics tests."

"I'm always interested in what you have to say, Melone."

"One of the Glock 9mm automatic pistols found in your house was used to kill Mark Fleming."

"So, they were in my office with Fleming?"

"Yes. But we don't think they had anything to do with each other. Just dumb luck that they were in your office at the same time. Fleming was sent by Becky Johnson to check your files. Wilson and Harris probably walked in on Fleming, hoping to find you, and Fleming ended up dead."

"Now what?" asked Gallagher.

"Somebody put a hit out on you, so we try to find him," said Wayne. "Who wants to see you dead?"

"Would you like a list?" Gallagher said.

"Whatever it takes to get us started," Wayne said.

"One more thing," interjected Melone. Now he was the one with the serious face.

"What is it?" asked Gallagher.

"We almost hesitate to tell you. It's a rather chilling thought."

"Like the thought of two guys waiting to assassinate me isn't chilling enough?"

"It's about Kate." Melone's words dropped like a bomb. Gallagher abandoned the humorous banter. He swallowed hard. His pulse quickened.

"Tell me," he said, almost dreading the reply.

"We found some papers in Wilson's bag."

"Papers?"

"Papers with information about Kate. The name of her business, the location of her office, and a description of her physical appearance. It seems like they had gathered all of this in advance so they'd know where to find her. We think she was their next target."

"Have you told this to Kate?"

"No. Thought we'd leave that to you. That is, if you think it will do any good to tell her. Maybe she's better off not knowing."

Gallagher was tormented by a mixture of escalating emotions: frustration—anger—revenge—his desire to protect Kate—the desperate need to uncover the sinister person behind these attacks on their lives. But a few of Wayne's words had triggered a thought in his mind—"put a hit out on you." He leaned back and looked up at the ceiling.

Of course ... now it all makes sense. It's Tauber from Las Vegas. I told the Feds last year that he was involved with that hit man, Johnny Nicoletti. The bastard is still after me!

Gallagher looked at Scott Wayne. "How good are your sources in Las Vegas?"

"We've got good sources everywhere. Why Vegas?"

"A year ago your compatriots at the FBI investigated a man named Lan Tauber. He has no official title, but he's some sort of special operative for the syndicates. I spotted him in Washington D.C., after he had dinner with Congressman William J. Prendergast. Sound familiar?"

Wayne nodded. "Isn't he the congressman who went to jail for bribery or some deal with the banking industry?"

"You've got it."

"What's the connection?"

"After I began asking questions about Prendergast and his possible involvement with three murders in New England, a hit man was dispatched from Las Vegas to get rid of me. Shot out the front tire of my car and ran us off the road in New Hampshire. Then came back to finish the job with a gun and a henchman a few weeks later."

"I heard about that from Dom," Wayne said. "You shot and killed the hit man in your apartment. They held your wife captive?"

"Yes, but his partner survived and made a plea bargain to save his ass. He told the police that a man named Jerry Murray had ordered the hit on me. The FBI never found Murray. In fact, no one in Las Vegas ever heard of him. They questioned Tauber for weeks and came up with nothing. I believe it now, and I believed it all along that Lan Tauber and Jerry Murray are one and the same."

"You think this guy Tauber sent the two goons from Chicago to kill you? Why would he bother? Wasn't that other case settled? The congressman went to jail. Technically, Tauber was off the hook," reasoned Wayne.

"You know how it works. These guys in the mob never forget. They don't ever want the word to get out that someone beat them. It makes them look weak. No, Scott, guys in that position always want to settle the score."

"Alright. We'll see if Tauber had any contact with Wilson and Harris. This may take some time. We don't want to let him know we're checking. Give us a few weeks."

"A few weeks? Come on, Scott, we don't have that much time. Are you sure you don't need any help?"

"I know you want to be involved. But, leave this to us. You've had enough excitement for a while. You just take care of your arm."

Typical bureaucrat! The condescending attitude scorched Gallagher.

"Right, and I'll keep looking over my shoulder for the next hood that Tauber sends after me," he said, bristling. "Remember, they wanted to kill me and they tried to kill Kate. I'm not going to sit here while you putz around and let that happen again."

Now it was Wayne's turn to seem miffed. "The last thing we need is a self-appointed vigilante. Stay out of this! Just give us a little time. We're on it."

Melone recognized the testy atmosphere that had developed and intervened in what Gallagher bet was his usual diplomatic style. "Scotty's a good man, Gallagher, he won't let you down."

"He better not. There's a lot at stake here," Gallagher warned. He darted a stare at Wayne but got no response. The FBI agent seemed to dismiss the admonition out of hand.

Melone stood up from his chair, signaling the end to the meeting. Then he flashed a knowing smile and pointed at his bedridden

friend with his index finger. "Remember, Gallagher, next time at the
Driftwood, and you're buying the drinks."

They left the room. Gallagher leaned back on his bed. He felt like
his blood was about to boil. *Do they realize what they're up against? Are
they going to get so hung up on procedures that Tauber will have the chance
to send someone else after us? I'll give them some time, but I'm not taking
any chances. I'm not going to let them do anything to hurt Kate. No...I'll
never let this happen again.*

Chapter Forty-Eight

It had been two agonizing, miserable weeks—in so many ways. Gallagher started the rehab on his injured arm. At times it was more painful than the bullet wound itself. His therapy was administered by a physical terrorist, three times a week. Stretching and retching. Adhesions tearing. But, gradually, he began to regain his normal range of motion. *Maybe the therapist isn't such a bad guy after all.*

He and Kate struggled, which was another source of pain. He tried to get close to her, but she pulled away, emotionally and physically. Their relationship—once so vibrant and electric—had become strained and distant, unplugged. The former perfect chemistry of their union now lacked an essential ingredient. He couldn't identify it. Gallagher was dying inside.

The incident with the gun had scarred Kate. She could have never dreamed—in her wildest moments—that she would kill another human being. Yet, she had fired three bullets into the back of a stranger. The police had questioned her extensively. The tabloids sensationalized the story. They dubbed her a modern-day Grace Kelly, the Quaker heroine who fired a bullet into the back of a bad guy and saved her husband, Gary Cooper, the marshal in *"High Noon."*

But other tabloid writers raised disturbing questions about the incident. One bullet, yes, but why two more? Self-defense or criminal intent? Why not a warning shot before she unloaded the gun into her victim? Had she taken on the roles of judge, jury, and executioner? Did the circumstances demand further scrutiny?

Kate hated the attention that was focused on her. Her privacy had been violated. She refused all interviews. Worse yet, for a while she feared being charged with manslaughter. Fortunately, the district attorney's office deemed it justifiable homicide. No charges were filed. No penalties imposed. But her psyche suffered. For the second time within a year she had been present at the scene of a shooting. Three men had died as a result of gunshot wounds. She had been a witness and a participant. Enough. She needed time to recover. Maybe she needed a way out.

Their time together was filled with emptiness. They tried to talk, but nothing worked. At times, they moved around the house like two lonely shadows. He never offered the details of the plots against them or the investigation that the FBI pursued in Las Vegas. He received almost daily updates from Scott Wayne, but there was nothing good. No developments. No links to Wilson and Harris. No rumors that Tauber had been involved.

Was this another dead end? Were they still in danger? He worried and stayed near her every moment, overreacting to every sound in the driveway, every knock on the door. No one would be allowed to hurt her again. He'd make sure of it.

"I'm going down to the store to do a little shopping. We need something for dinner," she said as she put on her jacket.

"I'll go with you," he said.

"No. It's alright. I can go alone."

"Kate, you don't understand," he pleaded.

"No. I'd rather be alone," she said flatly as she walked out the door to the garage.

Every day followed the same pattern. She asked for space—he wouldn't yield it. Yet they drifted further apart because he couldn't explain his overprotective actions.

For a while, he wondered why she stayed. He expected her to pack her things and say good-bye. But then he realized how concerned she was about his own recovery. While he still couldn't drive a car, she took him to his therapy sessions. She massaged his shoulder, applied his medication, prepared the meals or picked up a takeout order, did the laundry. She would never leave him alone in this condition.

Gallagher loved her now more than ever.

But he knew he was about to lose her, and he felt powerless to make her stay.

Chapter Forty-Nine

A few days later, the phone rang. It was Scott Wayne. Could Gallagher meet him at the FBI office in Government Center this afternoon? Without Kate. No details over the phone. Gallagher decided to drive himself. His arm felt better, even though his heart still ached.

He walked into the office. Wayne was sitting behind his desk. He looked somber. Gallagher frowned. This wouldn't be good news.

"How's your arm doing?" Wayne asked.

"It's okay. A few more weeks, and I'll report to spring training with the pitchers and catchers."

Wayne grimaced at the feeble joke. "Have a seat." He seemed impatient.

Gallagher sat down in the chair in front of the desk. Wayne avoided making eye contact with him. An uneasy feeling pervaded the room. Gallagher broke the ice. "Okay, Scott, the suspense is killing me. What did you find out about Lan Tauber?"

Wayne cut quickly to the chase. "Well, we went right to his office on our first day in Vegas. Figured if we started questioning anybody else, someone would tip him off that we were there."

"And?"

"Gotta give him credit. We showed up unannounced, flashed our IDs, and started asking tough questions as if we had more information than we were letting on. He was cool as a cucumber. He never clammed up and asked for his lawyer. He just denied everything. He seemed almost unflappable."

"How did he react when you mentioned Wilson and Harris?" asked Gallagher.

"Didn't even raise an eyebrow. When we told him we would subpoena phone and travel records, he didn't flinch."

"Did you get those records?"

"Yes, and they showed nothing. He never made or received a call from either one of them. The travel records of all the airlines out of Chicago did not have those two on any flight within the past year. If they made a connection with him outside of Las Vegas, they must have driven there."

"How about Tauber's travel records?" Gallagher pressed.

"Oh, he gets around, but there's no law against that. He's been to LA, San Francisco, Milwaukee, Washington ... lots of places. Interestingly, no trips to Chicago, so we couldn't even link him up with Wilson and Harris that way." Wayne flipped his pen onto his desk and gestured with both hands to indicate his exasperation.

"Milwaukee's only about an hour and a half from Chicago. He could have met them there," Gallagher reasoned.

"Yeah, but we had no way to prove it. We scanned the airport parking records for the date he flew into Milwaukee. The plates on neither Wilson's nor Harris's cars showed up. Tauber's alibi for the trip checked out. If he had a meeting with Wilson and Harris, he covered his bases so we'd never know. One thing we've learned about this guy ... he's a real pro. He didn't get this far by making careless mistakes."

"What's the word on the street?"

"Same story from everyone we talked to. He's a powerful guy, and nobody wants to mess with him. He calls the shots on all the dirty work the syndicate needs handled. Sort of a behind-the-scenes enforcer. When somebody mysteriously disappears in Vegas, our sources tell us that he knows all about it."

"Does he have a record?"

"Clean as a whistle...never been busted for anything."

"What's his background?"

"Started out in security for one of the casinos and worked his way up through the ranks. Next thing you know, he's got a big job that no one wants to talk about."

"Does he have an official title?" Gallagher asked.

"Special Operations, whatever that means. He draws a paycheck from a conglomerate that provides security services to the major casinos. It's hard to pin it down beyond that."

"Anybody ever heard of Wilson or Harris in Vegas?"

"No. The mention of their names was always met with a blank stare. Nobody knew them. They were Chicago guys and worked in the local underworld. They were definitely not big-time operators. If Tauber hired them, he must have had a connection in Chicago that set up the contact. But we checked that possibility extensively, and it was a dead end," said Wayne, as he motioned with his thumbs down.

Gallagher became restless in his chair. This is just what he had expected. The FBI had no sense of urgency in this matter. What did they care? No one was taking shots at them. He pressed Wayne harder. "So where do you go from here?" he challenged.

"There's nowhere else to go. We keep the case open and hope for a break. If Tauber's involved, he might make a mistake."

"I noticed that twice now you said 'if' he's involved. Let's get real. Who else could it be?" Gallagher's voice became more animated. His frustration had brought him near the boiling point.

"We have no other options here. Nothing else we can do," replied Wayne defensively.

"So what do expect me to do? Sit around and when the next hired gun shows up send you an email or call you on your cell phone?"

Wayne looked exasperated. Obviously, this conversation was going nowhere. He sought to end it by issuing a warning. "Look, Gallagher, that's why I asked you to come down here. You can't do what I think you're planning to do. If you go out there and put a bullet in Lan Tauber's head, you'll spend the rest of your life in the slammer or on death row."

"Maybe so, but at least I'll know that Kate's alive and safe."

"Be logical here," Wayne reasoned. "He knows the FBI has been questioning people and we're watching him. He's not going to take any more chances. He's bound to let this go. You should do the same. Let the natural course of events take over."

"Natural course of events? What's that supposed to mean?" Gallagher fumed.

"Eventually, guys in Tauber's position become victims of their own system. Think of it, the guy's almost seventy! He's made plenty of enemies over the years. Family members of people he had eliminated, other members of the mob, or even someone who wants his job. One day he gets popped, and they find him somewhere with a bullet in his head or a wire around his neck and life goes on in Las Vegas. That's how the mob polices itself. You and Kate live happily ever after."

"I can't count on that happening soon enough. What if you're wrong? What if he comes after us again before his time is up?"

"None of us have guarantees," Wayne said flatly.

"Bullshit! That's not good enough, Scott. We've got to stop him! If you can't do it, I will." Gallagher stood up. He wanted to reach out and grab Scott's collar and shake some sense into him about this gamble—this game of Russian roulette—that was being played with Kate's life.

Wayne held his ground with a defiant stare. But Gallagher felt Wayne was allowing him some room to vent his anger. In fact, Wayne's confrontational manner appeared to soften. He sighed and held his hands with the palms up, in a conciliatory manner. "Gallagher, I understand how you feel. I'm on your side, man. If I were in your place, I might feel the same way."

Then, his voice quickly shifted to make a stern point. "But, listen … listen carefully. If you go to Las Vegas and decide to take Lan Tauber out, I'm no longer on your side. The Las Vegas PD will arrest you, and I'm going to have to put you away. Now, that's not going to make me very happy. But, Brother, believe me, you'll spend the rest of your days in prison waiting for a lethal injection. I'm telling you … don't think of doing this. Go back to your wife. Let it go."

His last words were an emotional whisper—not just another warning, but advice from a person who truly cared.

Gallagher retreated. He sat down in the chair. He seemed wounded. What else could he do? Wayne's message had made an impact. Without any evidence, nothing could be done to Lan Tauber, at least not legally.

The other option meant throwing his own life away. Somehow he had to go on and still find a way to protect Kate. This had suddenly become his new mission, the singular purpose in his life. Keep her alive!

And, he had to do it alone. There was no one to help him.

Gallagher drove home slowly, oblivious to the traffic and sights all around him. His mind churned with thoughts of the incredible sequence of events during the past year. Johnny Nicoletti, Marcie Williams, Rebecca Johnson, Lou Wilson, Ben Harris, and now, once again, Lan Tauber—names associated with deadly threats to his very existence.

Only one menace remained. Could he do anything to remove it?

How his life had changed from happiness to uncertainty.

Was there any chance to rebuild his relationship with Kate? Would he be able to protect her from danger? Would they have to move? Go into hiding? Take on new identities and try to start all over again?

The future had become unclear. Gallagher had no idea where the next turn in the road would lead.

Chapter Fifty

Three Months Later

Lan Tauber awoke at seven-thirty in the morning and pulled back the vertical shades on his bedroom windows. He had a breathtaking view—lush green landscaping of the magnificent golf course framed by beautiful desert topography with soaring mountain peaks in the background. He loved living in Summerlin, one of the finest master-planned communities in the world with every cultural and recreational amenity imaginable. Right here in Southern Nevada, a short ride to the Las Vegas Strip.

Tauber was quite content with his life. He had everything: money, power, and connections. Especially connections. This made it possible for him to get virtually anything he wanted. Now in his late sixties, the thought of retirement had crossed his mind. But, why retire? He loved the action, and his job had plenty of it.

True, there were some distractions from time to time. The FBI had been dogging him for several weeks—interrogating him and questioning his friends about his association with two hit men from Chicago. But the investigators had gotten nowhere. Once again, they couldn't pin anything on him.

I'm way too clever for these rank amateurs. They're not going to get me for anything.

Tauber had completely stonewalled the FBI. He never admitted to knowing Lou Wilson and Ben Harris. He knew every avenue had been exhausted trying to link him to the two hired guns from Chicago, but the agents from the FBI didn't know what they were up against. Tauber thought things through in much the same way as the police. He knew how they backtracked every detail, looking for links to tie facts together and make a case based on circumstantial evidence. That's why the FBI could never prove that he and the two thugs from Chicago had ever been together. Tauber made sure that their car had not entered in the airport parking lot in Milwaukee where its license plate would have been time-dated by a security camera.

Details. He paid strict attention to details. That's how he had survived so long in such a ruthless business. But there was still one unfinished matter that monopolized his thoughts every day: Gallagher, the private detective from Boston, who was like a cat with nine lives. He had never met this character, but had to give him credit. Gallagher had managed to elude destruction on two occasions. It was highly unusual for anyone to escape Tauber even once. But twice? Unacceptable. Gallagher had earned a certain measure of Tauber's respect, but had also incurred Tauber's considerable resolve to make sure he never escaped again.

Tauber was a patient man. He had waited for the heat of the FBI investigation to die down. Now he had a new plan that would be carried out within a few weeks, as soon as he issued the orders. It was a foolproof way to rid himself of this persistent sore—an annoyance that had to be eliminated.

Tauber had his morning cup of coffee and prepared to leave for a meeting in Las Vegas. As usual, he was dressed impeccably—black slacks, a crystal blue blazer, black Armani shoes—all highlighting his perfectly combed white hair and his distinctive blue sapphire ring. He walked out to the driveway. It was another beautiful sunny day in Nevada.

He clicked his wireless access button to unlock the door to his silver Cadillac DeVille. He sat down behind the steering wheel and placed his key into the ignition. Suddenly, a powerful explosion erupted from the engine.

The windows shattered. Shards of glass sprayed into the car and viciously attacked his skin and face and pierced his eyes. He felt the flash of intense, burning heat as fire and smoke quickly engulfed the cabin. He let out a painful, agonized scream. But there was no escape.

The gas tank exploded. Within seconds, the tremendous force of the explosions and the ravaging fire had rendered him unconscious. The heat scorched his throat. He took his last breath. The fire raged on. The air reeked with the smell of burning plastic and human tissue.

A few neighbors rushed to the scene but were repelled by the smoke and fire. They stood back and looked on in horror as black smoke billowed from the charred wreckage and they realized the hopeless state of the single occupant of the vehicle.

Lan Tauber, the enigmatic power-broker from Las Vegas, could not be saved.

Epilogue

One Month Later

Her tail wagged excitedly. She panted. Her tongue darted side to side as she stared up at her master waiting for him to toss the yellow tennis ball again.

"Go get it, girl," he said, pitching the ball, damp with saliva and mud, to the far corner of the field. His form was good—harking back to his days as a pitcher for his college baseball team.

The beautiful golden retriever puppy, just four months old, sprinted gleefully away in hot pursuit of the bouncing, rolling object. She snatched the ball with a confident twist, lifted her head triumphantly, and then bolted back toward the man who had thrown it. She came to a sliding stop on the wet grass and dropped the ball at his feet. She barked once—almost begging—eager to start this game of fetch all over again.

Gallagher leaned down and took her head gently in his hands. "Good girl ... good girl," he said. Then he stroked her side, calming her down before resuming their playful game. He knew a lot about dogs, and this pure-bred golden was one of the smartest he had ever owned.

A man walked slowly into the field toward them, interrupting their private party. He wore an unzipped, three-quarter-length rain coat over his sport jacket. His hands were pushed forward in his coat pockets as he shielded himself from the brisk wind on this early April day. Yes, spring—but this was New England. Forty-five degrees with dampness that chilled you right to the bone.

Gallagher continued to crouch down and pet his dog as Scott Wayne approached. Then Gallagher stood and held out his hand toward her. "Stay!" he said. The dog dutifully obeyed.

"Could never get my dogs to listen like that," said Scott.

"She's real smart. Loves to play. Easy to train. Bought her from a breeder a few weeks ago."

"Beautiful dog."

"Yes. But something tells me you didn't come out here to admire my new pup."

"You're right"

"What is it?"

"Just wanted to ask you a few questions."

"Are these friendly questions, or do I need my lawyer?"

Scott smiled. The wind blew through his silver gray hair and pressed the ends of his mustache closer against his face. "Let's say this is a friendly visit. Off the record. I just need to satisfy my curiosity about something," he said gently.

"You're not foolin' me. One minute you Feds satisfy your curiosity, the next you go for an indictment."

Scott shrugged off his response. "I stopped by the house. Where's Kate?"

"Gone."

"For good?"

"Yes."

"I'm sorry."

"Had to happen. There was too much stress. Eventually the bond breaks. We just couldn't hold the pieces together."

"Maybe in time, she'll come back."

"I doubt it. I can't give her what she wants."

Gallagher leaned down and picked up the tennis ball. On cue, the golden retriever's tail began wagging excitedly. He stretched back and lofted a high-arching toss far across the field. The dog dashed off to get her yellow prize.

Scott looked on admiringly, but quickly returned to the serious discussion at hand. "You heard about Lan Tauber?"

"Maybe."

"I'll take that as an affirmative."

"You take it any way you want. I said 'maybe.'"

"Look, Gallagher, I told you once before. Tauber was a bad guy who hurt a lot of people and made his share of enemies. Eventually guys like him get paid back. Someone decides to get even; an old score is settled…"

Gallagher became angry and cut him off before he could finish. His voice exploded. "He tried to kill me twice! And my wife! He broke up our marriage and took her away from me. He deserved to die, Scott. You know it! Whoever killed him had a good reason and did the world a huge favor. I'm glad he's dead!" he said, nearly screaming. His jaws clenched. He glared at Wayne and then turned away. He fought to control himself from an even greater outburst.

"You're right," Scott sighed. He paused. His words hung there for a few seconds, a terse acknowledgment of Gallagher's emotional assertions.

But he looked as though he wasn't done, that the main purpose of his visit had still not been satisfied. He took a deep breath and exhaled. He raised his eyebrows and moved closer. "You know, a funny thing has happened."

"What's that?"

"Usually, in Vegas, when there's a big hit, the word leaks out. Sometimes it takes a few weeks, but eventually someone takes credit for the hit. Never officially, but with a little nod or a wink. It's sort of understood, almost like a rule of a game. But the boys in Vegas are stumped. No one has come forward. The street and the underworld are both very quiet. Nobody has a clue about the person or persons who put the bomb in Lan Tauber's car."

"One of these days, you'll find out. Maybe the History Channel will do a special on it."

Scott wasn't buying his cavalier attitude. "Gallagher," he asked in a deadly serious tone, "Did you do it?"

Gallagher said nothing. He leaned down, picked up the yellow ball that the dog had dropped at his feet, and tossed it again far across the field. Then he turned to face the FBI agent squarely. Gallagher's eyes narrowed. His demeanor became defiant. "What would I know about rigging a car bomb?" he asked. "I'm just a private eye."

Scott Wayne looked down at the ground and smiled, shaking his head from side to side, laughing quietly to himself. *Will I ever know what really happened? I should have known I couldn't break Gallagher down and get any information out of him.*

Wayne lifted his gaze toward the excited puppy running after the ball. "Great dog, you have there. What's her name?"

"Bernadette."

"Bernadette?" Wayne asked with a puzzled look on his face. "Where the hell did that name come from?"

"Oh ... I don't know, Scott, one day it just came to me."

CPSIA information can be obtained
at www.ICGtesting.com
Printed in the USA
LVHW02s0416231018
594506LV00001B/60/P